LEE's
HOLIDAY
SHOWDOWN

KEITH A CHARTERS

WWW.STRIDENTPUBLISHING.CO.UK

STRIDENT

Published by
Strident Publishing Ltd
39 Newark Drive
GLASGOW
G41 4QA

Tel: +44 (0)141 424 0092
info@stridentpublishing.co.uk
www.stridentpublishing.co.uk

A catalogue record for this book is
available from the British Library.

ISBN 1-905537-02-6 (10-digit)
and 978-1-905537-02-0 (13-digit)

Typeset in Utopia
Designed by Sallie Moffat

KEITH A CHARTERS

was born in Edinburgh and has since lived in Bearsden, Bedford, Harrogate, Bury St Edmunds, Edinburgh (again), Horley, London and Glasgow.

He studied Marketing and Law at the University of Strathclyde and should have gained a first class honours degree, but missed out by half a percent, mainly because he was playing snooker when he should have been revising for exams. (Let this be a lesson to all.)

After graduating, Keith worked for a large car manufacturer, an investment company and a healthcare company. Then, in 1996 he moved to London to work for a big, rather strange, financial company in which staff got paid for shouting at their customers and at each other. It was weird.

While in London, he started writing a lot. An awful lot. Soon writing was taking over his life, so he took a deep breath, gave up his 'proper' job and began writing full-time, having decided that that was what he really wanted to do with his life.

The 'Lee' series of books is the result.

Lee and the Consul Mutants topped the Children's Best Sellers list in the *The Herald*, with *Lee Goes For Gold* reaching no.4 in the same week.

As well as writing, Keith spends much of his time visiting schools. His presentations are renowned for making pupils and teachers laugh out loud. To find out how to invite Keith to visit *your* school, visit:

www.keithacharters.co.uk

ACKNOWLEDGEMENTS

My grateful thanks to the following:

New York Sallie, Alison Stroak and Graham Watson; Adriana Dunlay; Susan Pierce-Sloan; Mel; Murray and Daniel.

A special mention to my Aunt Edna, who recently discovered that Sallie, who edited this book, lived two doors along from her and her family as a toddler. She even managed to find a photo of Sallie kissing my cousin aged four. (See www.keithacharters.co.uk for details of this and other happy coincidences.)

And finally, apologies to the following for ruining, destroying or otherwise making a hash of some of their finer lyrics: the late, great Freddie Mercury (Bohemian Rhapsody, page 93); Stock, Aitken & Waterman (I Should Be So Lucky, page 92); and Peter Myers and Ronald Cass (Summer Holiday, page 15).

CONTENTS

This book is for:
Calum

Welcome to the world

ONE YEAR AGO ...

The rain was hammering down now, battering the sides of the tent as if gangs of kids were chucking pebbles at the faded blue and orange canvas. The noise was deafening and Lee was convinced he hadn't slept a wink.

Amazingly, his best friend Will still appeared to be asleep beside him, while Lee's four-year-old sister, Rebecca, lay on the other side, undisturbed by the noisy downpour. How? He had a quick look in their ears, but neither was wearing earplugs.

In fairness, this was only the first night in twelve that it had rained. The rest of the time it had chosen to ruin their *days* instead.

There had been one dry moment on the very first day of their holiday. Then, it had felt that this was the place to be; outside in the British countryside, admiring the view of the dingy campsite toilet block and being eaten alive by midges as evening descended. They'd played rounders for hours and everyone had joined in, including Lee's mum and dad and a couple of other kids on the campsite. Looking back, it was like a different holiday altogether – the sort he would much rather be on right now.

That had been day one. Days two, three, four, and right up to eleven had been dull (and not only in terms of the weather). Despite Rebecca endlessly repeating the appropriate ditty, the '*rain rain*' had refused to '*go away, come again another day*'. Tempers had frayed like tent canvas – partly because Rebecca had cheated during the 308th round of Eye Spy. Lee and Will had tried their best to find things to do in the confines of the tent, but it wasn't easy. Lee could now recite backwards all the words from the three comics he'd brought with him.

You hardly notice rain at home. When it rains, you escape inside, and when it stops, you run back out again. But with a tent when it rains, you curse a lot and have to cram everyone into a space the size of a single bed, watching as the plastic windows – windows that are hard to see through at the best of times – steam up.

He wondered if the rain would ever relent before they left for home. Twelve days down with only two more to endure. So not that long before they could return to the civilised world – a world of dvds, and gamestations; of frosty fridges rather than tiny cold buckets that turned things lukewarm; and of comfortable beds with duvets instead of thin, lumpy pieces of foam that left you with backache.

But perhaps most importantly, going home meant returning to the civilised world of houses, where whenever you needed a pee you didn't have to walk hundreds of miles to catch a bus to the toilets that hadn't been cleaned since the Romans left Britain and which were full of spiders, moths and daddy longlegs, all waiting to jump out at you.

How could you *not* need to pee when water was pouring down either side of the roof that was right above your head? It was like having 'Waterfalls, waterfalls!' shouted in your ear. And as soon as you start to think of water, your bladder immediately squeals, 'Okay, we're done! I'm full!' reminding you of the last very large drink you glugged the night before – one you gravely regret having had.

Sleep … sleep … Lee tried to convince himself. He

was as desperate *not* to have to go to the loo in this monsoon, as he was, in a different way, desperate *to* go. But it was no use. Images looped in his head – dripping taps, then gentle streams, then gushing hosepipes – until he just had to go or else there'd be an accident.

He fought his way out of his sleeping bag, like an escape artist freeing himself from padlocked chains while submerged in a huge tub of water. Both would drown if they weren't quick enough, but at least the escape artist would only drown in *water*. Lee's fate would be a lot less pleasant.

He eventually made it out of his bag and looked around for something to wear over his PJs. It was summer, but that didn't mean it was warm in the middle of the night.

Where were his clothes? In a neat pile at the foot of his bag where they were supposed to be?

Neat? No.

Pile? Yes.

He scrabbled around in the dark, trying to work out which were his clothes and which were Will's and Rebecca's. What he really needed was a police sniffer dog to help him out.

The more desperate be became for the toilet, the less he cared about whose clothes he wore. He just needed something – anything – to go over his PJs and keep him warm and preserve what little of his dignity was left. Having finally slipped into a top and pair of trousers that roughly fitted, and which may or may not have been his own, Lee staggered to the zipped door of the sleeping area, trying not to stand on the arms and legs of those around him. It wasn't just Rebecca and Will he had to watch out for; through a thin sheet that hung from the ceiling were the sleeping figures of his mum and dad (though it wasn't difficult to tell where his dad was; the foghorn snoring gave him away).

He reached around the sheet and grabbed the zipper that would peel back the flimsy fabric to reveal the main part of the tent.

Decision time. Unzip quickly, meaning a high-pitched zzz for a short period of time, or slowly, meaning less noise but a low-pitched zzzzzzz that would go on for longer.

Lee's bladder made the decision for him. *Quickly!* it begged.

Whose daft idea had it been to go on a crummy camping holiday anyway? Couldn't they have afforded a *good* holiday instead? Had every other holiday in existence been fully booked? Or had his parents finally given in to his constant nagging about wanting to spend fourteen days living in a tiny, smelly, cramped space without any modern conveniences?

Answer: none of the above.

No, Lee's parents had actually *chosen* this holiday. Out of all the holidays they could have had, and out of all the glorious, sun-drenched places on Earth they could have gone to, this was what they had opted for.

Why? What had they been thinking of?

Lee thought back over the last year. What had caused his parents to inflict this holiday on him? Had he done something really terrible? No, not that he could think of. Well, nothing they'd found out about (which was something altogether different). He recalled, as he unzipped the zipper, how his dad had described the holiday to him, after deciding that this was what they should do. 'Lee, you'll love it. It'll be an adventure! Just think of it – camping under the stars, fending for ourselves in the wilderness and cooking on a gas stove! We'll be like outlaws in the Wild West!'

'Did they have gas in the Wild West?' Lee had asked. 'I thought gas stoves were a more recent invention.

Unless they ate a lot of beans ...'

'Well maybe. But look, you know what I mean. We'll be at one with nature and with each other and ... able to spend lots of quality time together!'

Lots of Quality Time Together. That's when the alarm bells should've started ringing. It usually meant: *doing things we want to do but you'll hate*.

And that was exactly what it had meant for much of their holiday so far. The previous day was a prime example. They'd been dragged round what Lee's mum had insisted was a 'very *interesting* museum, honestly'. Or, as Lee had informed her on the way out, 'dorky rooms full of some old tat that the bin men forgot to remove'. Even Rebecca had nodded, although Will, who'd been dragged on holiday with them, could say nothing because you had to be polite to other people's parents.

And that Dork museum had truly been the *highlight* of the previous day. The rest had been spent looking around souvenir shops – or 'junk' shops, as Lee referred to them. They were full of stuff that was meant to remind those you supposedly loved of the wonderful time you'd had on your holidays while they had been stuck at home. Some people – presumably those with bad memories – even bought souvenirs to remind themselves of holidays they'd actually been on. If the holidays were that forgettable, why did they want to be reminded of them?

Well, if Lee wanted a reminder of this holiday, all he needed to do was buy a bottle of water. Or, if he wanted to save money, he could stick an empty bottle outside the tent because it would soon fill up with the drizzle that had dominated their stay. There hadn't been any clambering over rocks, nor hacking motorways out of nettled undergrowth with sticks (a particular favourite of Lee's when it came to woodland pastimes), nor hiding behind trees and scaring the life out of your parents by jumping out at them (causing several woodland birds to fall off branches in fright at the noise). At one stage Lee had been so bored that he'd actually found himself thinking that maybe school wasn't so bad after all! That's how fed up he was. How could he possibly think that spending time in the presence of his teacher, The Ogre, could be better than being on holiday?!

He soon found out.

Lee decided not to bother with socks – he would just jump straight into his shoes, which were sitting in the main part of the tent with everyone else's. He raised one foot and placed it beyond the sleeping compartment, onto the cold, black tarpaulin sheet that passed for a floor. Man, that tarpaulin floor really was cold! Cold in a cold-and-wet sort of way. A very realistic cold-and-wet sort of way. Lee placed his other foot forward. It, too, seemed to disappear under a layer of cold wetness. *The early morning dew must have sneaked into the tent*, he thought.

But the sound of his first proper step told him otherwise.

A massive Ker-Splosh.

Lee stopped in his tracks and looked down. Water. Gallons and gallons of it. Enough to reach up to his ankles.

'Aghhh!' he cried. 'Mum, Dad, Will, Rebecca! We're sinking!'

'Eh? What?' His dad's bleary face appeared from the sleeping compartment. 'What are you shouting about, Lee? It's the middle of the night!'

'Dad, look!'

One of Rebecca's pink shoes floated round a fold-up chair, bobbing along like a boat for the pixies emblazoned on its side. The whole tent was filled with water.

'Oh no ...!' his dad half moaned, half yawned, still lying down. 'This is all we need.'

'What is it?' It was Lee's mum this time. She looked a whole lot better when she went to work than when she woke up in the middle of the night. Her eyes were as baggy as some of Lee's jeans, and her face was the colour of a ghost that's seen itself in a mirror. Lee was glad he knew her, otherwise he might have thought he was having an extra-scary nightmare.

'Whatever you do, don't touch the sides,' Lee's dad said. 'You'll only let in *more* water.'

Lee doubted whether, even if he were to burst open a nearby dam, it would be possible to let in more water.

'What are we going to do?' he asked, his feet decidedly chilly and his bladder reminding him that it still needed to be emptied.

His dad dragged himself up out of bed. 'I can't believe this,' he mumbled as he pulled on his clothes (which, unlike Lee's, *were* located in a neat pile at the end of his sleeping bag). 'I've had it up to here with this rain.' He raised his hand to the top of his head in despair. 'Right, everybody up,' his dad ordered in a loud whisper. 'We need to bail out.' He stepped into the water that filled the main part of the tent. 'Look at this place!' Lee's dad dragged down the zipper on the tent's door and peeked outside. Even Lee wasn't ready for what lay beyond. Theirs was the only tent in that part of the campsite, alongside the river, and now they could see why. The river had burst its banks and they were now standing in a forlorn and flimsy blue and orange castle surrounded by a moat. Had the tent not been on a slight mound, it would have been under half a metre of water.

'The wellies,' Lee's dad said. 'Where are they?'

'In the car,' Lee's mum answered.

'Oh that's just great!'

By now, Will and Rebecca had both roused themselves. Will stuck his head out to survey the scene. 'I'm glad I can swim.'

'But what about the car?' Lee's mum asked, awake enough for practical concerns to be floating into her head.

'I doubt it can swim,' Lee said. 'It's never had any lessons.'

'Lee, that's not even remotely funny,' his mum told him. 'Especially at a time like this.'

'Sorry.'

Meanwhile, his dad grumbled as he had lifted the flap over the plastic window to give himself a view of where they'd parked. When he actually saw the car he said something else under his breath that we won't repeat here. The water was above the tyres but at least below the roof.

'Dad,' Lee asked, 'are we marooned?'

His mum's face lit up. 'Oh, now that's a good word, Lee.'

'Never mind good words. Yes, we are marooned.'

'Cool! Can we call the coastguard?'

His dad scowled. 'We're nowhere near the coast!'

'But if we were, then could we be rescued in a speed boat and hauled over the side by volunteers?'

'Maybe they'll send a helicopter instead,' Will stated, 'with a guy on a winch, so that we'll have to dangle hundreds of metres in the air as we're lifted to safety.'

'I refuse to be winched,' Lee's mum declared. 'It's never happened before and it won't start now.'

'We're not calling anybody,' Lee's dad said, not getting quite as excited as Lee and Will. 'But we do need to get out of here. I'll see if I can move the car.' He grabbed a jacket and waded outside.

Lee found it difficult not to laugh as he watched

through the window his dad making his way through the deep water. 'Watch out for crocodiles!' he called after him.

Getting to the car was easier than getting it open. Eventually Lee's dad hit upon the idea of climbing in through the window, using a brilliant device on his key ring that allowed the windows to be opened without the key being in the car's ignition.

'Woah!' Lee said admiringly as his dad's bum disappeared over the edge of the window. 'I always wondered why Dad's key let you do that. Whoever invented it must have been thinking of aqua driving!'

A head appeared at the driver's seat as Lee's dad righted himself.

'It'll never start,' Lee's mum said. 'The engine'll be flooded. And even if he gets it started, he'll never get it to move. The ground's too soggy.'

And she was right. The car had no intention of starting with an engine full of water. Five minutes later Lee's dad was back, having slid out of the car the way he'd got in. 'It's no use, someone will need to tow us out.'

'Are you *sure* we shouldn't call the Coastguard or the Air Rescue?' Lee pressed. 'I'm sure they could help.'

'I'm sure we can request some assistance closer to home,' his dad responded.

'I still need a pee, people,' Lee told everyone.

'Hold on until I get back,' he was told. 'I won't be long.'

'But I can't hold on. I'm desperate.'

'Then go round the side of the tent.'

'Everyone will see me!' Lee complained.

'Lee, it's the middle of the night. Who do you think will be looking?'

He had a point. So Lee waded out after his dad, who was setting off for the campsite owner's house.

Lee headed for the windowless side of the tent, checking the depth of the water with each footstep. He reckoned he would be up to his waist if he strayed more than a few metres from the canvas.

Lee heard his mum approaching just as he was in mid-flow. 'You okay, Sweetheart? How you getting on with your little jimmy riddle?'

'Arrgghh! I mean, much better, thanks!' Lee hollered before she came any closer.

When he returned to the tent, his mum got them all to roll up their sleeping bags and mats and put their clothes into plastic bags. She wanted to keep as many of their things dry as was possible. 'It's just as well this inner tent has a sealed bottom,' she said.

'Pity you don't have one too,' Will whispered to Lee.

Rebecca began to get upset at the thought of drowning. (Who wouldn't?) 'I'm smaller than everyone else. The water will get me first.' It was impressive logic for someone so young.

'Not unless the sharks do,' Lee joked, though no one else saw the funny side.

'Here,' Will said, comforting her. 'I'll give you a piggy back.'

Rebecca climbed up, and for a while she loved it. But, after several minutes, she remembered she got travel sick and was afraid of heights, which was good timing, because by then Will had tired of being kicked in the sides like The Lone Ranger's horse.

After another fifteen minutes Lee's dad returned. The campsite owner was with him and was doing a lot of fancy-pitching-your-tent-next-to-the-river-after-all-this-rain head shaking. Lee's dad tied a heavy rope to the car and slowly but surely the campsite owner's Land Rover dragged the vehicle up the slight incline, out of the water, like a dentist pulling on a particularly stubborn tooth. That done, the campsite owner untied his end of the rope and drove right up to the tent's front flap. The Land Rover was so much higher off the ground than a normal car that the water couldn't seep into it.

The owner jumped out, landing with a splash as his feet hit the sodden ground. He grumbled something about needing waders as he looked down and discovered that water was pouring into his wellies.

'This is Mr Cunningham,' Lee's dad announced, embarrassed. 'He's very kindly offered to help us out.'

It didn't look as if Mr Cunningham was being kind about it. He looked profoundly displeased at having been dragged out of his bed in the middle of the night.

'Right, everyone,' Mr Cunningham said, sounding slightly less gruff than he looked. 'Throw your stuff on board and let's get you out of here before the flooding *really* starts.'

'You mean it gets worse than this?' Lee asked.

'Has been known. A couple of years ago a honeymooning couple woke to find they were floating down the middle of the high street on their airbed. Stranded they were. Folks had a right laugh at them.'

'No way!'

'No, I'm only kidding.' (Lee had, of course, known Mr Cunningham was kidding, because what couple in their right mind would go camping on their honeymoon?) 'They didn't end up in the high street at all. The bed sank before it could get them there. It was freak weather like this though.'

Rebecca was worried by this. 'I'm scared of freaks,' she whined.

'Unusual weather, that's all Mr Cunningham means,' her mum explained. 'Anyway, you should be used to freaks by now after living with Lee.' She nudged Will, who grinned. Lee grimaced.

Mr Cunningham took charge. 'Right, leave the tent itself, but let's see if we can get everything else on board. Women and children first, mind.'

As Mr Cunningham lifted Rebecca onto the back seat of his Land Rover (probably wondering if it was safe to do the same with Lee's mum), Will said to Lee, 'This is brilliant!'

'Is it?'

'Too right! We're being rescued! We might be on the news.'

'Except that if we are, we won't see it. We don't have a TV, remember?'

'Yeah, but we can't stay here now, can we. So we might have to stay in a fancy hotel and it's bound to have TV. Maybe even a massive plasma screen that takes up a whole wall!'

'I bagsy the remote.' Lee said. 'And the staff will probably make us bacon rolls because they'll want to be really kind to us, since we've nearly drowned.'

'Trust you to be thinking of food,' Lee's mum interjected. They'd forgotten she was still in the sleeping compartment behind them.

'Mum,' Lee said, sticking his head in. 'Mum? What are you doing?'

'Shhhh,' she whispered. 'I'm putting on my make-up.'

'But why? You're only going out to the Land Rover.'

'I'm not letting anyone see me first thing in the morning without my make-up on. Now, you pass stuff out to Mr Cunningham while I get myself sorted out.'

Lee was about to argue, but then he remembered what his mum had looked like when he'd seen her without her make-up and decided that she had a fair point.

Will didn't get to stay in a fancy hotel, but he, Lee and Rebecca did get to watch TV as they sat in Mr Cunningham's front room. And, just as importantly, Mr Cunningham's girlfriend, Marilyn, managed to rustle up bacon rolls for breakfast at 6.30am.

Everyone was tired. Lee's dad sat shaking his head in disbelief that the quality time they were spending together was in someone else's front room. 'It is so humiliating,' he kept repeating to Lee's mum, who quickly fell asleep on the sofa.

Lee felt some sympathy for his dad, who'd had the notion that his children should be 'at one with nature'. It would have been good if they could have hugged trees, chatted to squirrels and caught their dinner, cooking it over an open fire and then eating it, just like people used to do thousands of years before the microwave was invented (presumably by someone with very small hands). But really, Lee was perfectly happy with his modern life. At no stage had he ever found himself hankering after a spell in the freezing outdoors, surviving by trapping and skinning cute bunny rabbits and digging up different kinds of roots. Mankind had invented supermarkets for a reason, and that reason was to make things easier. Why choose the hard life when a perfectly acceptable easy one with eye-level brand names was out there waiting to be lived? The world had moved on, and now his dad had to catch up.

Actually, his dad was thinking about moving on. 'We'll get the car picked up and hire another one to get home.'

'What about the luxury hotel?' Lee asked. 'With the plasma screens and free food.'

His dad shook his head. 'No point. All our stuff's soaking. We've nothing to wear tomorrow.'

'Couldn't we just sit around in our PJs and watch

telly?'

'I'm sure you'd just love that, but there's no point in paying to stay at an hotel if that's all you're going to do. You can watch our TV for free when we get back.'

'But ours won't be as big or as loud.'

'Also, the forecast for today is …'

'Let me guess,' Lee interrupted his dad. 'More rain?'

'You got it. What happened to the summer?'

'Another country stole it?' Will suggested.

Lee's dad shrugged. 'Maybe.'

The cartoon they'd been watching ended and Lee spun round. 'Dad, promise that next year we'll go somewhere hot.'

From her position on the sofa, where they all assumed she was still asleep, Lee's mum chirped, 'Oh don't worry. You bet we will.'

GETTING THERE

'*Oh, we're all off to sunny Spain, a viva spaghetti,*'
Rebecca sang, for only the eighty-seventh time since they'd left the house.

Lee's mum turned around from the front passenger seat. 'Rebecca, I think you're confusing your countries. Spaghetti comes from Italy, not Spain.'

'But you get yours at Tesco, Mum,' Rebecca replied.

'Ah, she's got you there,' Lee's dad said from the driver's seat.

'Yes, well, Rebecca, it's made in Italy and then they send it over here.'

'Remember back in the '70s,' Lee's dad said, 'they did that April Fool's thing on TV where they showed spaghetti growing on trees?'

'Oh yes,' his mum said. 'That was funny.'

'Why?' Lee asked. 'Why was that funny?'

'Because so many people believed it,' his mum replied.

Lee knew there were some pretty dumb people in the world, but he found it astonishing that they could be *that* gullible. They needed to get out more, even if only to the corner shop. One look at the packets would make it clear that spaghetti came from the ground. Where else would you find such long worms?

'*We're all going on a ... summer holiday. No more working for a week or two ...*'

'Mr Waters, would you mind putting on one of my CDs?' Will asked, nudging Lee and interrupting their driver's singing.

'Eh, well I guess so.'

Will checked that Mr Waters wasn't looking in the rearview mirror before pretending to wipe his brow with his hand and whispering, 'Close one!'

With Will's favourite CD playing, they trundled on along the motorway towards the airport.

'So, are you looking forward to your trip?' Lee's mum asked.

'Certainly am, Mrs Waters,' Will responded enthusiastically.

'Will, I'm quite happy for you to call me Fiona.'

Will blushed a bit. 'Okay, Mrs Waters.'

'It's good that you're able to come along again. I wasn't sure if, after last year' – she glanced at Lee's dad – 'you'd be so keen. Or if your parents would be, for that matter. But I suppose with the extension being built and whatnot …'

'Mum said it's perfect timing. It means the builders can make all their mess while I'm not there.'

'Yeah, but you won't get to see them knocking down walls with giant hammers and cool stuff like that, will you,' Lee pointed out.

'I'd much rather be going to Spain than seeing all that. You can see them doing that sort of stuff on those programmes about selling your house for more money than it's really worth.'

'That's true.'

'I'm not sure that that's quite the idea of those programmes …' Lee's mum said.

'Sure it is. You buy a scruffy old place, paint it and put in some really cheap fake-wood wardrobes, and then hope some sucker's prepared to pay a fortune for it.'

'Nice little capitalist we've got in the back there,' Lee's dad observed. 'I reckon you'll do alright when you grow up.'

'What's a capitalist?' Lee asked. He looked at Will but it was clear he had no idea either.

'Someone who believes in money, and in buying and selling things freely. Except not for free, if you get me.'

'No,' Lee said. Will shrugged, too.

'No wonder!' Lee's mum exclaimed. 'What sort of an explanation was that? I didn't even understand it and I actually know what the word means!'

Lee's dad took the hump. 'Well, go on then, you see if you can explain it any better.'

'Okay, I will.'

'Go on then.'

'Well, a capitalist is ...'

'A money grabber,' Lee offered. 'That's what dad usually says. Only he usually says "money grabbing ..."'

'Yes, yes, Lee,' his dad interrupted. 'I think that's quite enough on that subject.'

They were almost at the airport. A jet took off in front of them. 'Look!' Rebecca cried. 'A huge big plane.'

'Just like the sort we're all going to be flying on!' Lee's mum enthused. 'Are you looking forward to it?'

'Yes,' Rebecca answered. 'Will I get sweets on it?'

'I'm sure you'll get something nice.'

Lee fiddled with the cup holder between the front seats of the car and wondered what the point of it was. He'd never been allowed to use it in case he spilled drink all over the back of the car.

'This is already miles better than last year,' Lee declared.

'We're not even at the airport yet, Lee,' his mum pointed out.

'I know. But at least this year we're heading towards one. That's an improvement. No chance of a washout like last time.'

'It could still rain in Spain,' his dad noted before deciding that he needed to be more optimistic and adding, 'But I doubt it.'

They parked the car and hauled their luggage from the boot. Lee's dad eventually found a trolley and they stacked everything onto it, including Rebecca, who was allowed to sit on top like a fairy on a Christmas tree, even though Lee's mum thought it was a bit dangerous.

'Living is dangerous,' Lee's dad pointed out.

As they entered the airport, others were exiting, their holidays ended but tans topped up. Lee didn't understand why people were so obsessed with getting a tan. All your life your parents went on and on about making sure you kept clean, and then on holiday, they tried to persuade you that what you really wanted was to turn the same colour you spent all year trying to avoid going! What was the point of that? You might as well just not wash for a couple of months and save the money by staying at home.

Some returning holidaymakers weren't tanned; rather they were bright pink or red, like the colour of the flesh if you pull the skin under your eye out and then roll it over a bit, being careful to ensure your eye doesn't fall out as you do so.

The queue at the check-in desk was enormous, and Lee's dad wasn't happy about it. 'You don't get this on a campsite,' he complained. 'You just drive straight in, stick up your tent and hey presto, you're on holiday.'

'Do you remember how long it took us to put up that tent?' Lee's mum asked, and then answered her own question. 'Three hours. And that was just the poles. It took another hour to get the canvas on, and yet another hour to sort out the guy ropes and pegs.'

'Okay, so I'd never put up a tent before,' Lee's dad countered. 'It wasn't my fault.'

'But you did say – and I quote – that it "can't be that difficult, everyone else manages".'

'Yeah, but they've all been shown how to.'

'And when you went to borrow that ancient piece of moth-eaten cloth from your Great-Uncle John, did I not suggest that you got him to show you how to erect it?'

'Yes, but I …'

Lee was getting bored with this arguing. Was this what the whole holiday was going to be like? Plus, it was embarrassing with Will around. He interrupted his parents. 'Can we go off and play the machines?'

His dad looked at the length of the queue. It had barely shortened since they'd arrived. 'If your money's burning that much of a hole in your pocket, I suppose so. But mind and don't get lost.'

'Ace!' Lee cried, dragging Will away before Rebecca could harp on about wanting to go with them.

Airports can be great fun. Lee had been to one with his mum when his dad had flown back from somewhere he'd been working. The flight had been delayed for an hour and a half, which had become two hours, which had eventually become three. It had been boring waiting around and after two hot chocolates, Lee's mum had eventually relented to Lee's continual bleating about wanting to play a couple of the electronic games. It had been fantastic. Space wars; shooting, kicking and bashing things; and playing games you had no idea how to play, and which therefore used up your money very quickly, but were worth it because they looked really cool.

So Lee was very disappointed to find that this airport didn't have anything like the same range of games as the other one.

'What's this?' he complained to Will. 'One air-hockey machine, and one fruit machine we're not allowed to play anyway, and that's it!'

'Man, that's rubbish.'

And it turned out that the air-hockey machine was indeed rubbish and should have been put in the appropriate bin, because it wasn't working. A big *Out of Order* sign had been stuck to its playing surface.

'They're not joking,' Will said. 'Having such a poor selection of games really is *out of order*. We might as well go back to your parents.'

'Well,' said Lee, looking around, 'I suppose we could have one shot on the puggy.'

'The what?'

'The fruit machine. It's what my uncle calls them.'

'But we're not allowed,' Will pointed out.

'Well, technically, yes, we're not sixteen or whatever age you're supposed to be …'

'In fact, a long way from it.'

'Yes, but then also technically, no one's looking …'

Lee advanced on the machine.

'Do you think you should?' Will asked, concerned but advancing with him.

'One shot won't do any harm,' Lee said and reached up to stick a coin in. He was only just able to reach the slot by standing on his tiptoes at the side of the machine.

'Do you know how to play it?'

'I haven't a clue,' Lee said. 'We'll just press some buttons and see what happens.'

He pressed the buttons nearest to him and the reels spun round and round. Then the first one stopped. *BAR* it said. 'Do you get a free drink for that?' Will asked. But Lee was too busy staring intently at the machine to answer. The second reel stopped and another *BAR* came up.

'Is that good?' Will enquired.

Lee shrugged. 'It is if you're thirsty.'

And then the third reel stopped. It, too, said *BAR*.

'Three bars,' Will said.

'I can see that,' Lee told him. 'The question is: is it worth anything?'

'It doesn't seem to …' But Will stopped mid-sentence as the machine came alive with a clunk. 'What's that?'

Lee bent down and pulled out a round coin. 'Hey, we won something!' he said.

'One coin?'

No, not one coin, because the machine now coughed again, and then again, and kept on coughing, producing a coin each time.

'It must be broken!' Will said. 'It's like one of those hole-in-the-wall cash machines, the ones that sometimes give you more money than you asked for!'

Eventually, after almost a minute, the machine stopped. Lee looked around. Will looked around, too. Then they looked at each other. 'We're rich!' they cried.

A stern businessman, dressed in a pinstriped suit, looked up from his pink newspaper. He cleared his throat. Lee and Will faced the machine, trying to look innocent.

'Will,' Lee whispered.

'What?'

'Quick, fill your pockets.' Lee nodded at the booty in the machine's lap, then started scooping the winnings into his pockets. Will began doing to the same, whistling as he did so, as if nothing unusual was going on.

Just as Lee had picked up the last coin a hand landed on his shoulder, scaring him half to death. It belonged to the stern businessman.

'I don't think you should be playing that,' he growled.

'We're not,' Lee said.

The stern businessman raised his eyebrows disbelievingly. 'So what's in your pockets then?'

'Snotty hankies that I should have thrown away

ages ago. The green stuff's gone so hard now that the hankies are glued to the lining.'

The stern businessman didn't fancy checking this out for himself and turned his face away as if a bad odour was rising from Lee. (It was. It was the smell of fear.)

Lee and Will took this chance to escape. They ran in different directions, but both away from their inter-rogator.

The beauty about being a kid is that you can acceler-ate more quickly than an adult, even if you're so heav-ily laden with loot that the bottoms of your pockets polish the floor as you run. Of course, it helped that the stern businessman following Lee and Will had consumed one too many – or several too many – busi-ness lunches at whatever hotel he'd been staying in. He waddled after them for a few seconds but then thought better of it.

Lee kept an eye on where Will was running to and chased after him. Eventually he caught up.

'Man, that was close. We could have been in big trouble.'

'Yeah, but instead we're in big money!' Lee patted his trouser pockets, producing a chink as the coins bashed into each other. Will did the same thing.

'Come on,' Lee encouraged, 'let's see how much we've got!'

They found a quiet corner close to the toilet doors and grabbed a couple of seats. Lee emptied one pock-et, then the other. 'Woah!' He had to hold his eyes in so they wouldn't pop out of his head. Once Will had done the same there lay before them more treasure than Ali Babba had ever found in an Arabian cave.

But then Will noticed something.

'Lee, I've just noticed something,' he said, predict-ably. 'These coins … I've never seen any like them before.'

'Woah, maybe they're gold pieces like pirates used to own.'

'Used to "own" because they stole them from other people, you mean.'

'True.'

'But what are they? I've never seen anyone use one in a shop before.'

They each picked up a handful and inspected them. Will pointed to the inscription across the middle of the coins. 'It says here, *Token*.'

'Maybe these are the tokens of appreciation my grannies sometimes talk about.'

'No dummy, that's just a saying.'

'Aw.'

Will furrowed his brow for a moment. Out of the two of them, he was better at thinking and had all the actions to go with it because of the practice he'd put in over the years. Then his face fell.

Lee picked it up for him in case there were germs on the floor.

'What is it, Will?'

'I've just remembered. Those machines ... if you get a big win they don't pay you in money – hard cash – they pay you in tokens. And you have to change the tokens for money at the bar.'

'Okay, we'll go and change them then.'

'But we can't, can we. We're not old enough. They'll know we've been playing when we shouldn't have been.'

'Aw.'

'So what are we going to do?'

Lee checked his watch. 'Crikey, look at the time. We'd better get back or Mum and Dad will be gone without us.'

They scooped the tokens back into their pockets,

which were so full and heavy that they both had to hold up their trousers to avoid embarrassing themselves.

The queue had moved on quite a bit and Lee's mum was showing signs of anxiety.

'Where have you been?'

'Playing the machines. How come everything's moved so far.'

'They finally managed to drag someone away from their never-ending coffee break and got them to open another check-in desk,' his dad said. 'So the queue halved.'

'Next!' the check-in girl called without even attempting to smile, as if they were waiting to order burgers, not check in for their holiday flight.

'What's wrong with *her* face?' Will whispered to Lee.

'It's on upside down,' Lee answered. 'That arch-shaped scowl becomes a lovely smile if you turn it the right way round.'

'Yeah, but it would also be where her forehead currently is, so she'd probably lose her job for being too scary.'

All went smoothly at the check-in and they were directed to the departures lounge. Lee's dad pushed the trolley while his mum held Rebecca's hand so she wouldn't disappear, or kick any passersby if she mistook them for Lee's friends. They reached the security checkpoint and joined the queue.

'Please place any keys, phones, etc. into the small trays,' a security woman called out and Lee's parents dug into their pockets. Lee's dad went through first, then his mum with Rebecca, then Lee.

When the alarm went off, Lee thought there must be a fire but couldn't see any flames. He couldn't have set it off, not him, innocent purer-than-pure, butter-wouldn't-melt-in-his-mouth Lee!

'Would you step to one side please, Young Sir.' Lee

looked around him but there was no one else the guard could be speaking to. 'Any metallic items on you, Young Man? Anything in your pockets that you haven't taken out?'

'Eh …'

What was the penalty for smuggling fruit machine tokens out of the country? Death by hanging, firing or electrocution? Did you get a choice? No, no, this wasn't America, they couldn't do that to him.

'Anything to declare?' the guard asked.

Lee was nervous. 'Eh, well, I ate my sister's last packet of *Smarties* at Christmas, but she had so much stuff that I was doing it as a favour, to save her teeth, which are still young and vulnerable to decay …'

'I'm not interested in *that* sort of stuff.'

Uh oh! He was only interested in the really big stuff, the sort of stuff you didn't want to have to tell anyone about, ever, but which this man, whose eyes Lee could barely see because they were crammed so far up under his official-looking hat, demanded to hear.

'Well, an old lady once dropped some money on the bus and, well, although I picked it all up, I didn't actually give it all back to her,' he said shame-faced. 'I kept 10p for myself and bought some sweets with it. But I'm really sorry, I'll never rob a defenceless old woman again if you'll just let me go.'

Lee's mum was asking, 'What's up?' and Lee could see Will staring on in abject terror because he was going to have to go through the same machine.

The guard was shaking his head. Apparently what Lee had confessed still wasn't enough. 'I don't always brush my teeth?' Lee tried. 'I sometimes just use that mouthwash stuff instead to try to fool my parents.' He was running out of bad things he'd done in his life, or was it just that he was drying up with nervousness.

'How about you let me see what's in your pockets?'

Rumbled. There was nothing for it. Lee stepped to one side, stuck his hand in his pocket and emptied out the contents. His mum was goggle-eyed (though why she needed underwater vision equipment wasn't entirely clear). 'Where did you get all that?' she demanded.

Lee dropped his head but caught it before it hit the ground, upon which were splayed the feet at which he was now staring. 'Eh, I played the fruit machine,' he mumbled.

'Blimey!' the security guard said. 'You've had a lot more luck than me. I've put half my wages into that stupid machine and never won so much as a bean!'

'I've warned you before about gambling,' Lee's mum said.

'I'm really sorry,' the guard apologised.

'Not you. Him. Lee.'

'Oh, right, sorry Madam.'

'I know, Mum, but I only had one go. I didn't realise I was going to win … all this.'

'Or this,' Will called, emptying out his pockets before he too was caught and sent to spend the rest of his life in prison on the notorious island of Alcatraz, desperately longing for home and having to make do with occasional letters from his parents about how their extension was coming along.

The guard was still shaking his head. Lee wondered if a bolt had come loose in it. 'Well, you need to declare this stuff before you can take it through. Remember that for next time.'

So there would be a next time, they were being allowed to live. That was a relief. Lee didn't want to die until after their holiday in Spain. Preferably somewhere between ninety and one hundred years after it.

Lee's embarrassment had almost subsided by the time the plane was sitting on the runway. His dad had given him and Will a ticking off for gambling and had then taken the tokens off them as punishment. It was a relief really, because they weighed a lot and Lee was worried they would make holes in his pockets.

Lee asked his dad what he intended to do with them. 'Oh, I'll think of something,' his dad said, which meant he had absolutely no idea.

'You don't need to, I've already thought of something.'

'You, thinking this early in the morning?' his mum interjected. 'Well that's a first.'

'And what's your great idea?' Lee's dad asked.

'You could buy yourself and mum a drink at the bar over there.'

That seemed to go down well. It certainly brought a glow of expectant contentment to his dad's face. 'What a generous thought, Lee.' He stood up.

'And can you get Will and me and Rebecca something while you're there?'

The glow instantly disappeared from his dad's face. 'There's always an ulterior motive with you, isn't there, Lee.'

Lee didn't know what his dad was on about. Was ulterior somewhere between interior and exterior?

As it was, they didn't have time to buy anything. Their flight was called and they walked down the bouncy gangway to the plane.

'Taking off's the best bet,' Will said once seated. 'I love it when they lift the nose off the ground and you point up into the sky.'

Lee was less certain. 'I love it when you land and you know you haven't crashed and died in an explosion or in the sea.'

'Shhh! Stop that talk,' Lee's mum said from the row

behind. 'You'll make other passengers nervous.'

Right enough, the woman across the aisle from Lee was gripping the arms of her seat so hard that there was a danger of them breaking off.

The captain mumbled into his microphone something that no one could make out, but it was probably along the lines of; 'We're ready for lift off, so hold on to your horses everyone! Yeehah! Here we go!' and then they were charging along the runway.

Out of the window Lee could see buildings disappearing more and more quickly, then came that *up, up and away* moment when the front of the plane lurched up and they were sky bound. The woman next to him had her eyes closed, legs crossed and teeth glued together to stop them chattering with fear. (Okay, maybe not the last bit because it's dangerous to put glue in your mouth.) Lee reckoned the pilot had a secret camera somewhere and was watching this woman, because just as she was starting to relax a little, cautiously opening one eye and releasing her hold on the armrests to something less than a Vulcan death grip, he cut back the engines suddenly, causing her to double-check the straps on her personal parachute.

The plane eventually levelled out at its cruising altitude and even the most nervous passengers settled down. Minutes later Lee's dad said, 'Here come the trolley dollies,' and they all followed his gaze towards the cabin staff, while Lee's mum told off his dad for being sexist. 'For a start, two of them are men,' she said.

Rebecca was much less concerned with political correctness. She was hungry. As one of the female trolley dollies (Lee liked this name) approached, Rebecca stood up in her loosely buckled belt and shouted, 'Can you serve me first, please, I'm starving!'

The other passengers all laughed, as did the trolley

dolly. Rebecca smiled until her mum dragged her down into her seat. 'Rebecca!' she whispered reproachfully. But Rebecca knew how to milk a good audience and called, 'Make mine a hot chocolate with a muffin.'

However, Rebecca wasn't the only one feeling hungry. Other kids felt hungry too and weren't going to be outdone. 'Kit Kat for me!' one called, 'A Twix over here,' cried another and, 'I say, does one have any of those delicious but frightfully expensive Belgian chocs we normally have delivered to our house by courier?' asked a posh kid whose perfect family were seated around him.

'You'll need to take the marbles out your mouth first before Mumsy-Wumsy will let you eat them,' Lee muttered, causing Will to crease himself laughing.

The stash of confiscated tokens in Lee's dad's pockets was obviously making him feel loaded because he offered to buy them all something to eat and drink. 'Well, it's the holidays. I think we should treat ourselves.' So it was cakes and drinks all round.

Half an hour later Lee needed the toilet. He unbuckled his seat belt and swayed down the aisle to the front of the plane. There he joined three others in the queue. The door soon opened and out came a woman with a small child whose nappy had presumably just been changed. *Phaoh*, Lee thought. A couple of young kids nearby saw Lee's screwed up *oh man, that reeks!* face and realised what had happened. They nudged each other and pinched their noses with their fingers.

The queue soon shuffled forward and Lee approached the loo, sniffing gingerly as he stepped inside. Hmm. Nope, no worse than any other toilet, except that it was very dark and there was no light. How stupid was that! How was anyone supposed to aim properly without a light?

Still, he did his best. Indeed, he was still in the process of doing his best when the toilet suddenly became much lighter.

You might expect that Lee would have been delighted that he could now see what he was doing, or at least where he was doing it, but you'd be wrong. That's because when he glanced over his shoulder he saw an attractive teenage girl standing there. 'Oops! Sorry!' she said, blushing. If *she* was embarrassed, *Lee* was absolutely mortified, but there was nothing he could do. You can't stop peeing halfway through; there's no tap you can reach out to and turn off. So he had to finish what he was doing.

What now? Everyone would have seen the girl fleeing in terror down the plane's aisle. If it had been the rear toilet it wouldn't have been so bad, but he was in the one at the front, the one where, when you left, everyone could see you; everyone knew where you'd been and roughly what you'd been doing and, in Lee's case, everyone also knew he'd forgotten to lock the door and had let a girl see him peeing.

How long would it be until they landed? Could he stay in the toilet for the rest of the flight and hop off once everyone else had descended the steps onto the boiling Spanish tarmac? If anyone knocked he could make rasping sounds of the *I've-got-a-dodgy-stomach-you-really-don't-want-to-come-within-half-a-mile-of-me* variety. Would that work? No, because they always made you take your seat before landing, and a toilet seat didn't count.

It was a four-hour flight and they were only one hour into it. Three hours in a toilet you couldn't swing a mouse in, let alone any cat that was supposed to be chasing it. Not an appealing prospect. Maybe it would

be better to face the music (or any other form of entertainment that was being laid on) and put up with the
inevitable pointing fingers in order to spend those
three hours in the relative comfort of his allocated
seat, instead of one with a hole in the middle of it.

In the end, two things made up his mind. The first
was a knock on the door, with some guy calling, 'Come
on in there, push a bit harder if it won't come out! I
can't hold on much longer!' The second was a sudden
bump that sent Lee lurching forward. He managed to
grab a handle in front of him and kept his feet. (No one
else wanted them.) It was the toilet handle, and grabbing it made it flush. 'At last,' the voice outside said.
And then there was an announcement on the Tannoy
system. (Such systems are very aptly named, because
when they are used no one can hear themselves speak,
so they're clearly designed t'annoy everyone.)

'Ladies and Gentlemen, this is your chief stewardess
speaking. As you may have noticed, we're currently
experiencing some turbulence and the captain has
switched on the *Fasten Your Seatbelts* signs. Would all
passengers please return immediately to their seats.'

It was more what the chief stewardess *hadn't* said
that worried Lee. He knew what she really meant was:
*If you don't return to your seats and fasten your seat-
belts you're all going to die a horrible death. We've been
hit by fragments of a disintegrating satellite returning
to Earth that has chosen, out of all that vast, infinite
space out there, to occupy our tiny little area at exactly
the same time as us, hitting the plane, breaking a window and sucking out all of the air because of the difference in pressures, taking the passengers with it, just like
you see in those disaster movies. Still, don't worry, there
are worse ways to die ... although I can't actually think
of any right now ....*

Lee zipped up his fly and zipped out of the loo

(remembering to put the toilet seat down first – it was only good manners). He was soon straight past the man who was bursting for the toilet. As Lee pushed on down the aisle, everyone else was wishing they'd paid attention during the safety demonstration.

No one paid Lee any attention. They were too busy trying to ensure they didn't spill drinks over themselves as the plane bounced up and down.

Will looked up as Lee returned. 'Man, you were ages! I was beginning to think you'd fallen through the toilet and were hurtling towards the ground without a parachute.'

Lee stuck his head between his seat and Will's. 'What's with all the turbulence?' he asked his dad. 'Are the pilot and co-pilot having a fight over who does the landing?'

'No, Son, it's just instability in the atmosphere causing air currents that are gustier than normal.'

'Aw.'

'Nothing to worry about.'

'Unless,' said Will, 'you're thirty-five thousand feet up in the air.'

The anxious woman next to Lee who had a fear of flying and who, throughout the bumpy period of the flight, was not enjoying the turbulence one bit. She was muttering a prayer or ten. Actually, it was more like a conversation. Lee had only caught snippets of it. '*Oh Lord God … please save us … I'll give you all my money … yes, even the stash under the floorboards in my bedroom … I know I should have put it in a building society, but the rates of interest are so poor at the moment … Just don't let the plane crash … No, I don't think I should auction my collection of Princess Diana memorabilia and give all the proceeds to the Salvation Army. Ah, come on now, I think you're being a bit greedy there, God the all merciful, the all mighty, etc., etc. …*

Plus, to be honest, it's really not worth much these days, it's just a load of sentimental tat that I'm really quite embarrassed about having bought in the first place … The photos of Diana aren't even any good on most of the plates ….'

The woman was bonkers, Lee decided.

They didn't all die a horrible and tragic death. (Just as well, or this book would be a contender for *The World's Shortest Novel*.) Instead, they landed safely on the runway in Spain.

Through the window as they'd landed, Lee had been able to see the marvellous Spanish countryside laid out below, a countryside that was bounded on one side by the sea and a lot of hotels, and on the other side by mountains.

'Estamos en España!' Lee's mum said as they rolled to a stop.

'Oh, I forgot,' Lee whispered to Will. 'Mum thinks she can speak Spanish like a local just because she did it at school once.'

'That's good, isn't it?'

'Not really. She gave it up after a week, but she still thinks she's fluent, which isn't just bad, it's dangerous. She gets all her phrases mixed up, so we'll probably end up with a plate full of raw squid when she tries to order chips.'

'Yuck!'

'Exactly. So watch out. She'll be giving it *por favor* this and *grassy ass* that all the time, but she has no idea what she's on about. The problem is, she's convinced dad that she'll be able to act as translator for us all, and dad doesn't know any Spanish so he's only too happy to let her do the work.'

As they reached the door of the plane they were hit by a blast of hot air. Lee turned round to see if his dad was talking before realising that the hot air had to be coming from outside.

'Woah, it's roasting out there!' Lee told everyone.

'That's the idea,' his mum said. 'Would you rather it was like last year?'

'Definitely not.' Lee certainly preferred the prospect of a sun-drenched holiday to the memory of their rain-drenched one the year before.

Down the steps they went and into the terminal. Lee looked around, which didn't take long because the terminal was just a big empty shed without anywhere to eat or drink. His dad was also looking around, trying to work out which Customs channel they should go down. 'Does anyone have anything to declare?' he checked.

'Yeah,' Lee said. 'This airport is a dump.'

THERE

Their hotel turned out to be just what they'd all hoped for. It had firm, comfy beds, not the soft, overused-and-hardly-ever-replaced-by-the-stingy-owners ones you often got in bed and breakfasts back home. It even had a TV, although everything was in Spanish, making it rather difficult to follow.

Nonetheless, Will declared, 'This place is fantastic. Thanks for letting me come.'

'No problem, Will,' Lee's mum said. 'I'll bet it beats living in a house that's having an extension built, doesn't it?'

'You bet. With all that dust and mud around it's a real mess. No, I'm really glad to be here.'

'Well it's lovely of you to say so. And we're glad you're with us, Will, so you can help keep Lee out of trouble.'

'What do you mean, Mum? I never get into trouble.'

Before Lee's mum could answer, but not before she could give him a disbelieving look, there was a knock at the door.

'What's Spanish for *Who's there?*' Lee's dad asked as he went to answer it, Rebecca following behind him. Lee's mum didn't answer. She was too busy rushing to the bathroom mirror to check she was still presentable to whoever had come to see them.

Their guest was shown into the room. 'Eh, hello there everybody!' he said in a way-too-happy-to-be-normal voice, the sort that suggested he expected everyone to chant back: *Hello there! … whoever you are, you weird-looking person.* Maybe his parents were teachers and did this sort of thing with him every morning before doing it in their classrooms, or maybe he'd once starred in a pantomime. 'My name's Kevin and I'll be your holiday company representative for the time that you're here. Heh heh heh.'

Heh heh heh? What was that all about? He sounded like a car that wouldn't start in the cold. A very old car, the sort that should be in a dump with its wheels removed along with anything else that could be recycled. Lee feared that the closest Creepy Kev was ever likely to come to recycling would be when he repeated an old joke over and over in the very sadly mistaken belief that it – or he – might actually be funny. Lee looked at Will, who looked back at Lee and raised his eyebrows in amusement that this boy, who surely was on the run from school, was going to be their guide for the week.

'We'll be having a welcoming drink down in the hotel bar this evening at seven o'clock, heh heh heh, when we'll be telling you about some of the wonderful traditional and authentic trips and events we can arrange for you, and, a-heh heh heh, warning you of some of the dangers to avoid in the resort – the do's and don'ts, if you will, heh heh heh.'

'And our first don't,' Creepy Kev said, 'is …' He poised for dramatic effect but everyone just shrugged. Don't dye your hair using industrial strength toilet cleaner? It certainly hadn't done him any favours. Some of his hair was blonder than a very blonde Scandinavian, while the rest was darker than an underground cave with the lights out in the middle of the night. 'Don't miss the Welcome Party!'

'Aw.' Lee managed to rustle up slightly less enthusiasm than a man walking to the gallows to be hanged. Still, at least Creepy Kev hadn't finished that sentence with a …

'Heh heh heh. Eh? You get it? Don't miss the …'

'Yes, yes, we get it,' Lee's dad said. He didn't suffer fools gladly, or miserably for that matter; he just got rid of them. 'Goodbye. We may or may not see you later.'

'Heh heh …' The door was closed on Creepy Kev before he could annoy anyone further.

'I take it we won't be going to that party, then,' Lee's mum said quietly.

'Not unless anyone else wants to,' his dad said.

Lee thought for a second. 'Oh, I don't know. It could be quite … entertaining.' He winked at Will, who grinned back, even though he hadn't a clue what Lee was winking about.

'It might just be so bad that it'll be a laugh,' Lee explained.

None of the others were convinced.

'What have we got to lose?' Lee tried.

'Our sanity,' Lee's dad muttered.

'And aren't there usually free drinks at those parties?'

A glimmer of a smile crossed Lee's dad's face. 'Okay, well if you really want to go, I suppose we could tag along ….'

Even after they'd unpacked there was still plenty of time to explore their surroundings before the potential ordeal (as Lee's dad saw it) of the Welcome Party. Lee's mum would have been quite happy sitting out on their second-floor balcony for a while, admiring the view over the sea, but Lee, Will and Rebecca were all far too restless for her to be able to get any peace. So they headed down to the hotel lobby, where a few holiday-makers were playing pool while taking a break from the sun. Will spied an old Space Invaders machine that appeared to have been in the same spot since the year nineteen canteen. He nodded knowingly to Lee. They'd make their way back there at some point.

Next they came out to the swimming pool, with its two diving boards.

'Look!' Lee cried. 'How cool is that?!' He was pointing at the bar in the middle of the pool. People had swum out to it and were now sitting around in their swimming costumes sipping drinks.

'Alright!' Will said. 'Do you think they serve food there, too?'

'I doubt it. Can you imagine if someone dropped a hot dog into the water and you were swimming along and saw the sausage bit floating towards you like a giant number two? Or some chips with tomato sauce on them. It would look like blood. Everyone would be out pronto.'

As they passed the end of the pool, two teenagers climbed onto the diving boards to indulge everyone with a display of synchronised diving. After a count of three they stepped out along the board and, still checking what each other was doing, bounced on the end and leapt off. However, they hadn't decided whether to dive or jump into the water and, in the confusion, did half of one and half of the other. The result was an ear-splitting belly flop. They surfaced very quickly, howling with pain but trying to pass it off as laughter to those around the pool they'd been showing off to. They were fooling no one. As they climbed out of the water, Lee could see that their chests were a colour of red that not even the worst sunburn could have caused.

'Heh heh heh,' Lee mimicked Creepy Kev. 'That's so funny. Heh heh heh.'

Lee's dad found this amusing. 'I take it you haven't

much time for young Kevin,' he said.

'You must be joking, Dad. I don't think I've ever met a bigger numpty in my entire life.'

'Yes, when personalities were being given out he was definitely near the back of the queue.'

'Never mind,' Lee's mum said. 'I'm sure we'll be able to make our own fun on this holiday.' No one disagreed with that.

It was boiling, even in their T-shirts, shorts and flip-flops, and even though it was late in the afternoon. 'Can you imagine *working* in this weather?' Lee asked. 'Digging up the roads or something like that. You'd sweat so much you'd drown yourself.'

They reached the beach, which wasn't far from their hotel. It arced around the coastline, the longest continuous piece of sand Lee had ever seen. Brown, red and occasional pasty white bodies were laid out on clusters of sunloungers, while a few energetic holiday-makers were playing volleyball, leaping about on the hot sand.

Rebecca immediately set off for the sea, charging down the beach towards the water. 'Careful now, Rebecca,' Lee's mum warned to no effect. Rebecca sped up and, with proper sandals that didn't try to trip you up as you ran, was soon getting away from her parents. Lee, Will and Lee's dad ran after her. 'Rebecca!' Lee's dad called, but still there was no stopping her. He ceased trying to run in his own flip-flops because they were too loose and pulled up for a second to throw them to one side. He carried on in his bare feet. 'Rebecca, Love! You can't swim.'

Which was right, she couldn't, Lee now remembered. He increased his speed to try to catch up with the little tyke, but Rebecca was a fast runner. 'Don't go in, Rebecca! Stop!' he hollered, but still Rebecca made for the deep blue sea.

She made it to the edge and kept straight on in, her little legs kicking up water as she went.

'Rebecca!' Lee shouted desperately. 'Watch out for the killer sharks!'

Now that stopped her. It stopped her, turned her around and had her sprinting out of the water and back up the beach more quickly than you could say, 'Look, there's Jaws.'

Rebecca ran and ran until she reached her dad, jumped up into his arms and held on to him tightly.

And she wasn't the only one running. Lots of people had heard what Lee had shouted, and those who understood English were leading a sudden mass exodus from the water. Fear-stricken swimmers were making their way frantically for the shore. 'Agghh!' someone screamed as they fell off the inflatable bed they'd been lying on. It was enough to cause a wave of panic. Everyone assumed that the sharks had claimed their first victim. Parents leapt off their sunloungers and sprinted for the water to drag their children to safety. And the lifeguards, who had been enjoying a quiet game of cards, stood helpless, unsure what to do because there were so many people running in different directions. A few people who thought they couldn't swim suddenly found that they could, because it was the quickest means of escape.

'Whoops,' Will said as Lee's mum caught up with them.

Lee's mum was watching the chaos unfold in front of them. 'Quick, Lee, we'd better get off the beach before anyone realises it was you.'

Lee thought this was a good idea. Indeed it was probably the best idea his mum had ever had, because he really really really really didn't fancy having thousands of angry holidaymakers chasing after him, seeking to tear him limb from limb in an orgy of violence the likes of which one normally only found in cartoons and computer games.

Lee beat an anonymous retreat. For starters, he pulled off his red T-shirt so that no one would recognise him because of it. Had he been carrying a false moustache he'd most probably had donned that, too, although it might have been rather unconvincing given his age.

Lee's dad took off the cap he'd been advised to wear to protect his bald spot. ('What bald spot!' he'd argued, though not for long once a mirror had been produced.) 'Here,' he said to Lee. 'I think you should wear this for now.' Lee thanked him. Anything to make himself less recognisable. 'Eh, I think maybe we should try the promenade to find somewhere to eat for later,' Lee's dad suggested.

'You kids can choose what to eat tonight and which restaurant we'll go to, and Dad and I will choose tomorrow night,' Lee's mum said.

'Thanks, Mum!'

'Yeah, thanks Mrs Waters.'

'Fiona, remember.'

'Okay, thanks.' Using her first name just didn't seem right to Will.

'I want pizza,' Rebecca chirped.

'I think the boys should choose tonight after all the trouble you've just caused, Young Lady,' her mum said.

'That's not fair,' Rebecca complained.

'Oh, I think it's perfectly fair,' her mum told her in no uncertain terms. 'I think we'll need to keep you on a lead like a dog if you're going to run off like that all the time.'

'Pizza's fine by me,' Lee said, feeling kind of sorry for Rebecca. His sister really knew how to pull the heartstrings, with her sad, moping face and I'm-so-hard-done-by eyes. 'Yeah, me too,' Will agreed.

'We come all this way across the continent to Spain and what do you guys want? Pizza. Exactly the same thing as you eat at home.'

'But Dad, we like pizza.'

'But you might also like something from Spain that isn't pizza if only you'd give it a try. You might even like it *more* than pizza. Who knows! All that sea out there with all those fantastic fish in it!'

'Just waiting to be caught in big nets, then sliced up for us to eat. Mmm, yum, Dad. No, I think we'll stick with pizza tonight, thanks.'

Lee's dad held up his hands to indicate that he'd tried his best to persuade them. 'You don't know what you're missing,' he told them. 'Calamari, paella, chorizo …'

'Which team do they play for?' Lee asked.

His dad shook his head. 'Okay, I give up trying to broaden your cultural horizons.'

Although it was still early in the evening a few of the restaurant owners were out trying to drum up business. They were smooth operators, Lee noted. 'Ah! You are so beautiful! I would love for you to grace my restaurant with your presence. It would attract so many other customers if you were to sit with your family at one of my tables.' Lee's mum loved this sort of attention. 'Ah, Señor!' she would say, pretending to be modest and blush while lapping it up for all she was worth.

Lee and Will were perfectly happy with the first place they came across. It sold pizza and that was all that mattered. But Lee's mum was much more fussy. They passed on several perfectly acceptable restaurants because she was always able to dream up something that wasn't quite right about them, but the others all knew she was just trying to get another owner to flatter her. Still, it was her holiday too, so they allowed her to indulge herself for a while until eventually time forced a decision upon her. 'So, where are we eating?' Lee's dad said to his wife. 'Although I thought that Lee and Will were supposed to be making this evening's choice.'

'That's fine by me,' Lee's mum said. She turned to the two boys. 'What do you think? I thought that first place was perfectly good, didn't you?'

Lee smirked. 'You mean the one with the good-looking owner who said you were the most attractive woman he'd ever seen in his entire life, since the very first day his mother had held him in her arms? That one?'

'Eh, did he say that? I don't really remember …'

'Hello everyone. My name's Angela, and the first thing I'd like to do is welcome you all to Spain. I'm sure you'll have a wonderful time here as me and my colleagues will be around to help you make the most of your stay.'

The woman speaking to them was a witch, Lee was quite certain of it. Admittedly she was younger than your average witch and lacked a black pointy hat, but she had black hair and was surprisingly pale for someone who lived and worked in a hot, sunny country. Plus, she had that haggard look that all witches have, the result of staying up late at night so they can howl at the moon after trying out dodgy potions. And, Lee noticed, in the corner of the bar there was a broom propped up against the white wall. It was unlikely that it was ever used for sweeping.

'In a minute I'll be outlining all the lovely trips you can go on to the lovely places in the lovely surroundings. And if any of you lovely people do go on them I'm certain you'll have a lovely time.'

'How lovely,' Lee's dad mumbled over the top of his wine glass. He took a sip and made a face. 'What *is* this stuff?' he asked no one in particular. 'It tastes like … like rats' tails.'

Rats' tails! It was one of the witch's secret potions, something she'd concocted in her cauldron earlier that day!

'The first of our trips is our totally traditional and authentic Spanish mountain fiesta night,' she hollered so everyone could hear.

'Traditional my …,' Lee's dad began to say, but was cut off by Lee's mum hushing him so she could hear what the witch was saying.

'First we'll go up into the mountains at the back of the resort to a traditional up-in-the-mountains restaurant, where you'll be served up an enticing array of authentic Spanish food. Whilst eating you'll be serenaded with some traditional flamenco guitar music. Unfortunately, our usual guitarist, Estaban Jo, broke his arm the other day after one of his goats gave him a traditional butt up the bahooky while he was practising, but I'm delighted to say that we've managed to find someone just as good to replace him, so Dave Smith will be serenading you with his traditional flamenco guitar playing.'

'Dave Smith!' Lee's dad mumbled again, incredulous. 'Very Spanish!'

'Shhh!' a woman at the next table whispered. 'Some of us are trying to listen.' She had the look of a stern headmistress from a snobby girls' school – not a good look to have as far as Lee's dad was concerned.

However, that was Lee's dad told off, and he sat and drank his disgusting secret potion in mopy silence, making faces at the moany woman when she wasn't watching him.

This was not at all out of character for Lee's dad. He didn't like authority and when it reared its ugly head (*especially* ugly in this woman's case), his instinct was to fight against it. He liked the idea that he was a rebel, even now in middle age, even though there was nothing rebellious about his life. Wife, two kids (okay, admittedly no dog), a nine-to-five job, a couple of holidays each year …. However, old photos of him – photos he tried to keep hidden, but which Lee's mum had once secretly shown Lee (well, it was a secret until Lee started slagging his dad off about them) – revealed a younger dad (in fact, not a dad at all at that point) with really bad sticky-outy, frizzy-wizzy-let's-get-dizzy long hair. There was even one of him playing football wearing a manky red, white and blue headband to keep the hair out of his eyes. He wouldn't have looked out of place in a heavy rock band. (Actually that's not true. He'd have looked very out of place because he couldn't play any instruments, although having listened to some of his dad's old records – yes, records, not CDs – Lee wasn't sure that a lack of musicianship would really be that much of a hindrance.)

The witch carried on. 'Then, once you've eaten as much as you possibly can, which is, of course, the Spanish tradition, we'll pour you back into the bus and bring you back down the mountain …'

… to our secret coven where I and my fellow hags will turn you all into frogs and newts and other quaint, if rather slippery and slimey, pond life, Lee was thinking. Because by then you'll all be so stuffed and tired that you'll be unable to resist our wily witchy ways.

They'd better watch out for this woman.

Maybe she realised she'd been rumbled because she was handing over to someone else. 'Now, I'd like you to meet Kevin, another member of our staff, who'll tell you about one of our other fun and exciting traditional trips.

Lee had been wondering when Creepy Kev would get a shot at making a complete idiot of himself (something his mother had already done by giving birth to him).

'Eh, hello there everybody!'

A few people were clearly too shocked by his idiocy to think, and called back, 'Hello Kevin.'

'Heh heh heh,' Kevin laughed, mistaking himself for a cabaret act.

Lee looked over at Will. 'Heh heh heh,' they went together, causing Lee's dad to snigger. Unfortunately, he tried to keep his snigger in so it wouldn't become a laugh and annoy old Fish Face at the other table, but it's never good to keep things in, you should always let them out (like burps – both the mouth and bottom varieties), because if *they* don't come out something else will. In Lee's dad's case it was a large bogey, which blew down his nose into that strange channel called a philtrum that links your nose with your upper lip so that, when you're young, you don't have to pick your nose to get your snotters, you can just wait for them to run down into your mouth. Mmm, delicious!

'Oh gross!' Lee's mum exclaimed. Fish Face flashed her a harsh, severe stare, while Lee's dad grabbed a hanky and wiped the bogey onto it.

'The special traditional event I want to talk to you about is, heh heh heh …'

'Heh heh heh,' Lee and Will echoed again.

Creepy Kev seemed to find this funny. 'Heh heh heh,' he laughed, looking around to see who was mocking him.

There was nothing for Lee and Will to do but repeat him. 'Heh heh heh.' They looked away to make it more difficult for Creepy Kev to realise it was them.

'So anyway, what we'll do is we'll take the bus to

a traditional down-on-the-beach restaurant, where you'll be served up an enticing array of authentic Spanish food. Whilst eating you'll be serenaded with some traditional Spanish spoon playing ...'

Lee's dad couldn't hold back. 'Spoon playing!' he exclaimed.

Creepy Kev heard his comment and responded. 'Heh heh heh,' he went (echoed by Lee and Will), 'Eh, yes. Unfortunately, our traditional maracas player, Fonda Mashakers, was poisoned the other day while he was practising. A rattlesnake mistook his maracas for a potential mate. But I'm delighted to say that we've managed to find someone just as good to replace him, and so Canteena Cutlery will be serenading you with her, eh, traditional Spanish spoon playing, heh heh heh.'

'Heh heh heh.'

'Anyway, it'll be a marvellous, fun evening, and then afterwards we'll go down onto the beach for games like, heh heh heh,' (cue echo), 'like sticking your head against the end of a brush handle, running around it lots of times until you're incredibly dizzy, then trying to run in a straight line. Heh heh heh' (you get the idea by now), 'it's so funny watching everyone falling over and whatnot, heh heh heh. So make sure you book into what will surely be one of the highlights of your holiday with us.'

'Can we do that one?' Rebecca asked. 'I want to see you fall over, Dad.'

'I want to see your dad hold a brush handle,' Lee's mum told his sister. 'That would be a first.'

Creepy Kev stood back and let the witchy woman come forward and speak again. 'And finally ... oh, and that's perfect timing, because here she is, just in time to join us ... it's Samantha to tell you about our final featured event.'

'Hel-lo there!' Lee's dad said under his breath as Samantha stepped hurriedly through the door and joined the witch. Never were two women less alike. A steamroller would have been hard pushed to flatten the creases in the old hag's face, whereas Samantha looked like an air-brushed advertisement for a 'keeps you younger – always' face cream with her soft, youthful skin and luscious eyelashes. And whereas the sorceress had hips that could easily support a crumbling towerblock, for several days if necessary, Samantha was svelte and appeared very fit.'

'Dad ...' Lee said.

'Yes?' his dad responded without taking his eyes off Samantha, and without even blinking, lest he got less of an eyefull of her.

'Put your tongue back in.'

'What? Eh? Oh, ha ha ha.'

Will and Lee looked at each other. Was this a new, dangerous strain of Creepy Kev's laugh? Was it contagious? They didn't echo him, just to prove to themselves that they hadn't succumbed to whatever spell the witch had cast on Kevin. Had Kevin come out to Spain a normal young man, one who wasn't a cretin or an idiot, but under her influence rapidly become a total imbecile?

Lee's mum was less interested in the laugh than in why her husband's eyes were hanging out of his head and bouncing around on long springs, like in cartoons. He ought to have had eyes only for her, yet there he was ogling slinky Samantha. 'She's not *that* good looking,' she said. 'See,' she pointed, 'she's got a small scar on her left knee.'

Lee's dad leaned forward and stared hard. 'Where?'

'I can see it quite clearly,' Lee's mum said huffily.

Lee could tell why his mum was jealous. Not only was Samantha fabulous looking, but he could just tell that when she opened her cute mouth she was going to have an incredibly sexy voice, like the women in the James Bond films: deep and husky and …

… and not at all what Samantha actually sounded like.

'Awright there? Are yous all enjoying yourselves wi' the wine and that, aye?'

'Oh no, she's Scottish!' Lee's dad said, horrified, as if Scottish people still weren't allowed over Hadrian's Wall, let alone into Southern European countries such as Spain.

Samantha was oblivious to Lee's dad's disappointment and carried on, her rasping voice sounding as if she smoked three hundred duty-free cancer sticks a day. 'Well, what A'll be tellin' yous about th' day is the do's and don'ts around the resort. Or the do's and dinnaes, as they're called where A'm fae.'

Several holidaymakers were staring blankly at each other and whispering about needing a translator. 'Can you speak Spanish so we can understand you!' one called out.

'Hoy you, shut it, Pal' Samantha joked. 'Right, now there arenae many of these here dos and dinnaes, so listen up. The first do is: do go an' look around, 'cos there's loadsa places to see and a' that. The second do is: do go on one of they trips what Kevin and Angela were tellin' yous about a minute ago. They really are pure dead brilliant by the way, and really great value for money, too – and that's comin' fae a Scot an' a'!

'Now then, the dinnaes are more important, and the first one is: dinnae go swimming unless yous've checked to see there's water in the pool. A bit obvious, I know, but yous'd be surprised. They pools outside are, despite what yous may have heard, actually cleaned once in a while, and we did have one bozo who went for a midnight swim when there wasnae any water in the pool. Needless to say, he didnae drown, ha ha ha, but he got one hell of a sore nose when he dived in. So be careful of that, okay.

'Now, the second dinnae is: dinnae eat the seafood til it's dead, 'cos it can be a wee bit nippy otherwise, know what A mean?

'Third, and this is definitely an important one, too: always use the stairs or lifts tae get tae yer rooms. Dinnae climb up the balconies or drainpipes, 'cos you're no Spiderman, know what A'm sayin', and if yous fall you'll end up doing yersel's in big time.

'So, a few important dos and dinnaes there for yous. That's all fae me, so have a fandabbydozzy holiday, aye!'

'Fandabbydozzy!' some nutter called out.

'Aye, go yersel', Big Man,' Samantha shouted back.

Witchy Woman returned to the front once again. 'So there you go folks. Any questions? Anything we can help with just now?' She cast her eyes as if they were spells and found someone at a table on the far side of the room, hidden from Lee's view by a pillar.

'Yes, excuse me,' a man's voice said. 'How does one upgrade to First Class on the trips you have outlined?'

'Eh, upgrade …?'

'Yes, to the better seats on the transportation you provide to take one to the events. I wish to ensure my family travel in comfort and style.'

'Well we don't actually have First Class seats on the buses, just standard seats.'

'Really? Well that is rather disappointing. It was bad enough being in cattle class on the plane.'

This didn't go down well with the other guests. 'Hey, who are you calling cattle?' someone called, while someone else shouted, 'Stuck up toff!'

There was much muttering and pointing in the

direction of the family who acted as if they were too good for everyone else – The Perfects as Lee decided they should be called. Not that they seemed to notice the barracking directed at them, although now that the Welcome Party was over they were quickly gathering up their belongings and leaving.

The rest of the Welcome Party guests made for the door as soon as they had finished their free drinks. It didn't matter that the drinks were disgusting; they were free, and that was reason enough for finishing them.

'What a rare treat that was, eh?' Lee's dad said. 'Good to know we'll be in such good hands throughout the holiday.'

'Heh heh heh,' Rebecca chirped, managing a remarkably good imitation of Creepy Kev.

'They were terrible,' Lee observed. 'The worst presenters I've ever seen. They'd never get a job on TV.'

'Right, I'm starving,' Lee's dad declared. 'Let's go and eat. I've no doubt your mum wants to be flattered again by Mr Smarmy at that restaurant.'

Lee's mum was too busy rummaging through her handbag to respond immediately, and by the time she finished, Lee's dad was leading the way to the seafront restaurants.

'Ah, Señora! Welcome back. You are looking quite ravishing tonight. And your daughter! Isn't she gorgeous! She looks good enough to eat.'

'Be my guest,' Lee offered. 'Although I think you'll find she's got a bit of a kick.'

'And your funny little son. He's got such a great sense of humour.'

'I must have,' Lee told Will. 'I'm in this man's restaurant while he's swooning all over my mum.'

They were shown to their table, the owner still fussing over Lee's mum like a first-born grandchild. A waiter, who was clearly taking lessons from the owner in how to be a smoothie with the ladies, but whose English wasn't quite so fluent, approached their table.

'Good evening,' he said. 'Devante Manuel.'

'No thanks,' Lee's dad said. 'We know how it all works. Just the menu, thanks.'

'Que?' said the confused waiter. 'Devante is my name. Devante Manuel.'

'Oh, sorry,' Lee's dad said, realising his mistake.

'I get you drinks, yes?'

'Yes, please.'

'What you like?'

Lee's mum and dad ordered a carafe of wine (no relation to a giraffe, which can hold a lot more wine than a carafe).

The waiter turned to Lee, Will and Rebecca. 'And lovely children, what you like?'

'A sick bag,' Lee mumbled, having read some of the weird stuff on the menu.

'Que?'

'A 7-Up, thanks.'

'Okay, and you, Young Lady?'

'I've already …' Lee's mum began before realising he was addressing Rebecca, who chose the same as Lee; as did Will.

'A clean sweep,' Lee's dad observed.

The waiter was puzzled again. 'You think floor is dirty? I cleaned it one hour ago.'

'What? No, no. It's fine.'

'You're confusing him,' Lee's mum said. 'Maybe I should have a go. I'll ask for some water for the table.' She turned to the waiter. '¿Dónde puedo conseguir mi coche mantenido?'

'At the garage up the road,' the waiter replied.

This didn't seem to be the answer Lee's mum was expecting, but she said, 'Oh, thanks,' anyway as Devante departed to get their drinks, scratching his head as he went. Lee hoped it was confusion, not fleas.

When their meal came it was delicious. Lee and Will did their best to eat the enormous pizzas placed in front of them, but they just couldn't manage. Rebecca didn't even eat half of hers.

'I'm going to explode,' Will declared.

'Try to do it quietly, please,' Lee's mum said, chewing on the last of some chicken.

'I think we'll have an early night tonight,' Lee's dad said. 'That way we'll be in good shape to get up at the crack of dawn tomorrow and make the most of the day.'

Lee's mum wasn't so sure about the getting up at the crack of dawn bit. 'We're on holiday. We're here to relax. There's no point in coming away if we're not going to chill out.'

'But if we wanted to stay in bed all day we'd have been better off staying at home and saving our money,' Lee's dad argued.

They had this same argument every holiday. Lee reckoned that if his dad could have his way he'd spend his week's holiday on a muddy army assault course, whereas his mum would spend it sitting in a sauna at a health spa, having her nails done. However compatible they were as parents, they weren't compatible when it came to holidays.

'What are we going to do tomorrow?' Lee asked.

'Read a book by the pool,' his mum suggested.

'Boring,' Lee told her. 'Unless it's a really good book, like that *Lee Goes For Gold*. Remember that one?'

'The one with all the money on the cover?' Will

checked. 'I read that, too. It was awesome. Mind you, did you see the picture of the author in it? Have you ever seen anyone more ugly?'

'Well, reading by the side of the pool is what I'd like to do, and it's my holiday too,' Lee's mum insisted.

Lee's dad certainly wasn't enthused by the idea of book reading. 'That's what I do at home every night. No, I want to do something more active. Swimming in the sea, windsurfing, water skiing, or paragliding or …'

'What's paragliding?' Will asked.

Lee's dad was only too happy to explain. 'You get a parachute strapped to your back, then they fix a rope from your waist to the back of a speedboat, which pulls you along until the parachute lifts you up out of the water and way up into the air.'

'Sounds scary, doesn't it,' Lee's mum said.

'Not at all,' Lee's dad countered. 'It's as safe as houses.'

'Houses sometimes fall down.' Lee said. 'There was a story about one on the news a couple of days ago.'

'That's just a saying,' his dad said. 'Anyway, what's the worst that can happen? All that's underneath you is sea.'

'Yeah, but it's a *long way* underneath you. Remember what happened to those guys diving off the boards at the swimming pool? That hurt. So imagine if you were falling from hundreds of metres up in the sky.'

'That's not going to happen,' his dad said.

Lee wasn't convinced.

'Anyway, I'm not saying I'm going to do that, it's just an idea. I'll probably do windsurfing instead.'

'Can we do that, too?' Lee asked.

'We'll see.'

Devante Manuel brought the bill – or 'the William' as Lee's dad called it.

'I don't get it,' Will said.

'Bill is short for William,' Lee's mum explained.

'Is it?' Lee asked. 'Isn't Will short for William?'

'No,' Will said. 'At least that's not what my name's short for.'

'What's yours short for, then?'

'It isn't. It's just Will.'

'So Will's not short for William.'

'It can be.'

'But yours isn't.'

'No.'

'So why's Bill short for it then? That doesn't make any sense at all.'

'I don't know,' Lee's dad said.

'Aw. But …'

'Just leave it, yeah?'

The night-time sounds of the resort were very different from the quiet in Lee's house once he'd gone to bed. Now he lay listening to the layers of noise: the background of twitching insects; the regular crashing of the waves; the rasping of mopeds and motorbikes being driven up and down the road; and the singing and shouting of revellers heading out to, between or back from, restaurants and clubs. It was a different world from the one Lee was used to, however he was enjoying it already.

DAY ONE

They all awoke early the next day, not because of the sun streaming through their windows, nor because of the local birds making a racket to greet the day, but because Lee's mum was screaming like a mad woman.

'Agghhh!' she yelled from the bathroom. 'Get it out of here, get it out of here!'

Lee's dad leapt the entire length of the bed. 'Fiona, what is it? Are you alright?'

'It's a cockroach! It's huge and it's in here! On the floor!'

Lee, Will and Rebecca were all in the other bedroom. They heard Lee's dad open the door and then turn around again, back into the bedroom. 'I'll be there in a second. I'm just putting my shoes on.'

By this time Lee was out of his bed. He decided to follow his dad's lead and squeezed into his trainers, though only after bashing them on the ground first to make sure no cockroaches had climbed inside overnight. He'd seen a programme on TV about how redback spiders in Australia could climb into places like shoes, and you could die from their bites (the spiders, that is; shoes generally aren't all that vicious), so it was best to be careful.

He joined his dad outside the bathroom.

'You'll need to open the door, Fiona,' his dad called to Lee's mum.

'I can't,' she shrieked back. 'I'm on the toilet.'

'Can't you lean over and reach the handle?'

'I'm *on* the toilet! Standing on the seat! If I lean that far forward I'll fall off and break my neck.'

'Where's the cockroach?'

'Under the sink.'

'Can't you run past it.'

'I hate them, they're horrible things. I don't want to be in the same room as one. They're almost impossible to kill. Even if you stomp on them nothing happens. And they're highly resistant to radiation and would probably be the only creatures to survive a nuclear holocaust. I read that somewhere.'

Which was impressive and interesting – if somewhat depressing and useless – information.

'But, Fiona, I wasn't thinking of dropping an atom bomb on it. Anyway, I can't help unless you open the door.'

'There was another shriek from inside. 'Aghhh! It's moving again.'

'Where? Where's it moving to?'

'It's moving to … to the door!'

Lee and his dad both leapt back about three metres in one go, not keen to come face to face, or even feet to face, with this monster.

'I wish I had my old hiking boots with me,' Lee's dad said. 'They weigh a ton. I'd like to see this cockroach after one of those landed on its head. It might be able to survive radiation, but I'd bet a million pounds it wouldn't survive one of those boots.'

By this time Will and Rebecca were on the ends of their beds looking out at what was going on. 'Is it out yet?' Will called.

'Not yet … aghhh, there it is!' Lee leapt onto Will's bed. He had no intention of remaining on the floor while there was any danger of that thing being down there.

It was the most horrible, disgusting creature Lee had

ever seen. Its long antennae waved about in the air as it skittered across the floor. It's body was just as repulsive; oily-looking and sleek.

Rebecca whimpered. It was all that Lee could do to stop himself doing the same thing.

Although the cockroach was skittering, Lee could see what was on its back.

'It's got wings, Dad. Can it fly?'

It seemed his dad hadn't considered that, because he backed off another step. 'I think they can. Although I've never seen one flying before.'

'What are you going to do, Dad? Are you going to stamp on it?'

'I'm not sure if that will work.'

'It's worth a try. What else can we do?'

'Call the manager!' Lee's mum hollered from the bathroom. She opened the door cautiously and peered around it. They could all see that she had a towel wrapped around her feet just in case the cockroach decided to retreat into the bathroom again.

'No, no, I'll deal with it,' Lee's dad said, trying to act like he was taking the five-centimetre-long insect in his stride.

'Pick it up and throw it over the balcony!' Rebecca encouraged him.

'The last thing I'm doing is picking it up,' he assured everyone.

The cockroach skittered some more, and Lee could feel some skittering of his own coming on as it drew closer to him. Then it stopped and Lee's dad summoned up the courage to make his move, kicking it as hard as he could against the wall. The cockroach slammed into the skirting, but righted itself as if nothing had happened and sprinted for the safety of a cupboard. Boy, those revolting insects could certainly move when they wanted to. But Lee's dad was having none of it. He had the taste of blood in his mouth (from where he'd bit his lip when he'd kicked) and wasn't going to let the ugly little sod get away. He swung his foot again, sending the beast out into the open kitchen, and then jumped high in the air, landing both his heels right on top of the creature.

Rebecca and Lee's mum looked away, but Lee and Will stared intently to make sure it was dead.

'Oh yuck, look, half of it's moving! It's left the other half behind!'

This was too much for Lee's mum. She closed the bathroom door and was sick.

Lee's dad set off after the escaping head half. With only two legs left from its original six, the cockroach wasn't moving quite so fast now.

'Come here you little ...'

Lee's dad brought down his shoe again. Thwack! This time there was no sign of anything sliding out from under his shoe, but he ground his heel hard into the tiled floor anyway, just to be certain he'd finished off the not-so-little blighter.

'Hasta la vista!' he declared triumphantly.

'Do you know what that means, Dad?' Lee asked.

'No, but it sounds good, doesn't it?'

'It means goodbye,' his mum called.

'Isn't it a shame it's not waving to us as it goes,' Lee's dad said. 'They're very ignorant those creatures.'

After wiping up the squashed mess that was once a cockroach, it was time for breakfast, followed by a mad dash to the pool to get a decent space. It was busy. Very busy. So busy that you had to have very thin legs to be able to squeeze between the bodies already lazing by the side of the bright blue water.

'You see, this is why we need to get down here nice and early,' Lee's dad pointed out, delighted to be proved right for a change.

Lee's mum had a huge bag of towels with her. 'Right, these are for lying on, and for drying yourselves off after you've been swimming.'

Drying yourself off, Lee thought. What an original use for a towel. His mum was obviously more of a genius than he'd realised.

Lee's dad went off in search of some sunloungers and managed to locate two, which he squeezed into a spot that was currently in the shade but which would, according to his precise astronomical measurements, soon be sun drenched. Lee's mum carefully placed her towel over the blue plastic and lay down. 'Oh, yes, this is more like it,' she said. 'This beats work any day.' With that she picked up a book and started reading.

Meanwhile, Lee's dad was sorting himself out. He placed his book at the end of his sunlounger and laid his towel across the middle section.

'Dad, Dad! I want to go swimming!' Rebecca cried. 'Armbands, armbands!'

'Okay then.' Lee's dad stood up, reached into the towel bag and took out a set of bright orange armbands. 'Here you go, Rebecca. Right, let's get these on you. Come over here.' The excited Rebecca did as she was told. Lee's dad sat down heavily on the end of his sunlounger, the bit nearest the pool. The sunlounger's two sets of legs were towards its middle, so sitting at the bottom was, Lee's dad instantly discovered, a very bad idea. His backside sank to the ground and the top end of the sunlounger pinged high into the air. Of course that was the end on which he had, moments earlier, placed his book … the same book that now flew through the air towards the swimming pool, pages flapping and fluttering with joy at their new found freedom,.

'Aghh! My book!' Lee's dad attempted to save his paperback, rising athletically from the ground and leaping to catch it before it became something interesting (and mushy) for children to dive to the bottom of the pool for.

Lee watched as his dad, who had been a useful goalkeeper in his youth, stretched out a hand, grasping for the elusive book. Would he save it? Would he manage to touch it round the post to great applause from the crowd? Or, in his desperation to save a book that he'd bought for 50p at the school book fair, would he fail to notice the young woman walking along the poolside?

His hand got a firm grasp of the book just before the point when its well-fingered pages and grubby cover passed the point of no return (or certainly of no *dry* return), only for him to trip over the young woman's leg and into the water. The young woman was taken completely by surprise. She wobbled. She teetered. She cried, 'Agghh!' And then she, too, fell in. Lee's mum sat up to see what all the commotion was about. There in the pool before her was Lee's dad, his book held proudly aloft and a lot drier than he was, and a young woman who was ... who was Sexy Samantha, her rival in romance.

Lee's dad had only just realised what had happened and was mortified. 'Oh, eh, Samantha, I'm so sorry. I was just trying to save my book.'

Samantha flapped her arms and spat out a mouthful of water. 'Aw man, look at ma clathes. They're wringin'! What did yae hauf tae go and dae that fur?'

'Pardon?'

'What's the story?'

'I was just trying to save my book. It was going to get soaked.'

'Book? I'll book yeh. Could y'have no just let it fall in

instead a' shoving me in an' a'?'

Of course everyone else around the pool thought this was hilarious. It was the stuff of those TV shows on which people only do really stupid things when they happen to have a video camera running.

Lee's mum didn't have to say anything. She was delighted to see that Sexy Samantha was now Seething Samantha, who would have been even more irate had she not been a holiday rep who had to try to be polite to the guests. Maybe this would teach Lee's dad a lesson: that something would go horribly wrong if he dared to look at other women.

Lee's dad climbed from the pool (after first throwing his precious book onto the *middle* of his sunlounger), then gave Seething Samantha a hand out. Had she been in her bikini, things wouldn't have been so bad (and Lee's dad would have enjoyed the experience more), but she was in her full official holiday-rep gear – skirt, blouse, blazer and shoes.

'Honestly, if there's anything I can do …' Lee's dad offered.

'I think you've done enough damage as it is,' Lee's mum stated. Samantha seemed to agree. Lee's mum stuck her hand in the pool bag and then said to Samantha. 'Here, take this towel to dry off. You can give it back next time you see us.'

'A'll need tae go 'n' change anyway,' she said, slipping her jacket off. She squelched towards the hotel building, wrapped in the towel and dripping her dignity as she went.

Lee hadn't hung around when he'd seen this unfolding. Along with Will, he had quickly jumped into the pool and swum to the other side so that he wouldn't be associated with the idiot who had accidentally pushed the sexy rep into the water.

But his mum now realised she'd forgotten to tell

them something and called them over.

'What is it?' Lee asked after swimming back.

'You need to put sun cream on.'

'But we're swimming just now. There's no point.'

'That's even *more* reason to put it on. The water refracts the sun's rays, and so intensifies the impact of the solar radiation it emits.'

'Aw.' Lee was beginning to think his mother was turning into a nuclear scientist. First it was the radiation-proof cockroaches, now solar radiation.

'You'll get melanomas if you don't put it on.'

'Mel who's?'

'Melanomas.'

Lee didn't fancy having to use the sun cream of a girl he didn't know, so he went along with his mum's demands. Will clambered out with him.

'You'd better dry off first,' Lee's mum said. 'No point in putting it on while you're wet. Here.' She handed them each a towel. Lee opened his up.

'Aw Mu-u-um! Look!' Lee held his towel out before him.

'What?'

'Look at it!' I can't use that. I'll be humiliated.'

'That's a good word,' Lee's dad said, impressed with his son's vocabulary.

The only word Lee was interested in was the one emblazoned across his towel: *Tweenies*.

Will was laughing. That was until he unfolded his own towel. 'Aw, Mrs Waters …'

'Fiona, remember, Will. Anyway, what's wrong with them? They're only for drying yourself.'

'But, Mum. *The Tweenies* …' Lee said.

'And *Barney* …' Will added, showing her his own towel, with its picture of the cuddly purple dinosaur blob.

'There's nothing wrong with them!'

'Mum, were these a bargain?'

'Yes!' she replied, pleased with herself.

Lee's mum was well known for her bargains. She couldn't resist them. It didn't matter that what she bought was nearly always completely useless junk, just so long as she got it for a bargain price. Whenever she came back from a shopping trip she would always say, 'You'll never guess what *I* got!' and the rest of the family would reply, 'Yes, we can. You got a bargain,' for it was the same every time.

'Mum, *The Tweenies* and *Barney* … they're for kids half our age, if that.'

'But they were two for the price of one.'

'No wonder! I wouldn't have taken them for free! They're terrible and embarrassing. Haven't you got any others?'

'No, I thought you'd be happy with those ones.'

So there was nothing for it but to use them, although obviously with the stupid, childish pictures on the inside, closest to their bodies, to make it more difficult for everyone else to see them. They also dried off very very quickly.

Sun cream on, they leapt back into the pool. There were plenty of other children about, including some roughly their own age and older. Soon they were involved in a game of international water polo – Britain versus Scandinavia. It was exhausting, having to keep afloat all the time in the middle of the pool and then swim frantically to try to get the ball. And then, when you did get it, some great Dane (though not the dog variety) or Swede (not the vegetable) or Fin (not the shark kind) or Norwegian (not a people named after anything remotely funny) would half drown you trying to get the ball for their side. After half an hour Lee and Will were both shattered and decided to withdraw so they could recharge their batteries.

Rebecca took this opportunity to join them, climbing down the steps into the shallow end and doing doggy paddle to reach them. Eventually she made it.

'I want to play with you,' she said.

'Well okay, I suppose so,' Lee agreed, not relishing the prospect, although at least it would tire them out less than water polo. 'What shall we play?'

While Rebecca and Lee sorted out what to play, Will dived under the water and through Rebecca's legs. She laughed and, when he came up to the surface, said, 'Do it again, do it again!' Will did it again … and again … and again … pretending to be a dolphin because Rebecca loved those.

It was on Will's seventh or eighth dive that Lee noticed Rebecca's face change temporarily.

'What's wrong?' Lee asked.

'I needed the toilet,' Rebecca said.

'You mean you *need* it.'

'No, I *needed* it.'

'You … Oh no, Rebecca, you haven't … That is *so* gross!'

Lee could feel the water around him suddenly that little bit warmer. He backed off rapidly.

However, it wasn't himself Lee was thinking of. Poor Will was, he could see, at that very moment passing beneath Rebecca's legs, his hair swirling back as he pushed forward.

Will surfaced and laughed. So did Rebecca. Lee didn't.

'What is it?' Will asked, seeing his friend's straight face.

Should he tell him? Should he reveal that Will had just swum through Rebecca's pee without a full-face mask to protect him? Or was it better to leave him in blissful ignorance so he wouldn't contribute to what was already in the pool by throwing up?

'Nothing,' Lee said, deciding that, on balance, it was better that his best friend didn't know the truth. 'I'm just a bit tired. I think I'll go and have a lie down for a while. You coming?'

Will hummed and hawed, his humming definitely more tuneful than his hawing.

Lee tried to persuade him and wracked his brain for something to say. 'It's best to have regular rests, otherwise you'll get sunstroke,' he tried.

'Eh? What difference will resting make if you're still lying out in the sun?'

'Yes, you're right, that's why I'm going to … eh, to play pool inside,' he said and was relieved to hear Will say, 'Okay then, I'll give you a game.'

Lee insisted that they both rinse off in the showers, even though the water from them was freezing cold compared to the pool. 'Why's this so important?' Will asked. 'My parents never make me do this.'

'Ah, well, they should. It gets rid of all the, eh, bacteria that you can pick up in pools. They cling to you and can make you horrendously ill. Can kill you, in fact.'

'Can they?'

'Sure.'

'So how come most kids go swimming and are perfectly alright?'

'Because they have showers afterwards.'

'I thought they put chemicals in the water to protect you against the bacteria. Isn't that what makes your eyes sting?'

Lee had, by now, had long enough under the cold shower and was certain they must both have washed off what had seeped into the water they'd been swimming in, so he was willing to concede. 'Yeah, maybe you're right. Come on, let's get dried and play pool.'

It was the shiny suit that Lee noticed first as he and Will hung around the pool table.

'Never trust a man in a shiny suit,' his dad had once told him when they had watched a film together, and, sure enough, the man with clothing that glinted like silver foil had turned out to be the baddy.

However, there was more to this man's dodginess than just his suit, even if it did make you want to wrap potatoes in it and cook them on a barbecue. His eyebrows met in the middle and were a different colour from what little remained of the hair on his head; his crooked smile made it look as if he was worried about half of his teeth falling out; and his tie looked as if it was made out of snakeskin.

'See that guy?' Lee whispered.

'The one with the really bad nose hair?'

'Eh, I hadn't noticed that. Maybe. The one whose suit is more silvery than the inside of a flask.'

'Yeah. Plus he's wearing sunglasses, even though he's indoors.'

'Eh, no, my guy isn't wearing sunglasses.' And Lee now realised there was another Mr Shiny at the far end of the bar.

A man and a woman were busy trying to outdo each other at the pool table, one bad shot following another. It was looking as if the table might need to be re-covered by the end of the day. Will placed a couple of coins on the side of the table to book the next game. Meantime, Lee was a few steps ahead of him, heading back to the bar to take a closer look at the Shiny Brothers.

Now the differences between his description and Will's were clear. Will's Mr Shiny was younger and taller than Lee's and had three women holding on to his every word, whereas the man Lee had spotted was standing alone, casting an eye over the place.

Will caught up with Lee. 'What are you doing?'

'I'm just taking a look.'

'What at?'

'Those two guys.'

'Why?'

'I don't know. There's something … something strange about them.'

'They're like security guards.'

That made Lee stop and think. 'That's exactly what they're like – bodyguards for someone important.'

'They might have guns hidden under their suits.'

This worried Lee. He took a step back towards the pool table, but not before he spotted the hotel manager approaching the Mr Shiny who was standing on his own.

'Are you wanting to play?' the woman called from the pool table.

Lee spun round jumpily, as if having been caught spying on someone.

'Eh, have another game before us if you want,' he said.

Will waited for the woman to turn back to the table before whispering, 'Why did you let them have another game?'

'I want to see what's going on.'

'Well, the woman is much better than the man. He's either letting her win or is the worst player in the world, because she's completely useless but somehow still won that last game.'

'Hmm, right.'

'You're not really listening to me, are you?' Will said.

'In a minute,' Lee muttered, eyes still focused on the hotel manager and Mr Shiny. 'Hey look, they're going off.'

'Who are?'

'What?'

'Lee, you're talking to yourself.'

'The hotel manager and that man are going somewhere.'

'And …?'

'Let's follow them.'

'Our money's on the table for the next game.'

'Bring it with us.'

'What? Then someone else will get in before us and …'

'We might find out what's going on.'

'Is something going on?'

'I don't know. That's what I want to find out.' Lee walked backwards to the pool table. 'Are you coming?'

Will shrugged. 'Okay then.'

Lee took a few cautious steps into the lounge. Will followed and after a few more steps they were heading towards the hotel's reception and the fancy foyer. They were in time to see Mr Shiny enter the manger's office and close the door behind him.

'What do you think they're discussing?' Will asked.

'I don't know. I wouldn't be able to tell even if I could hear them, would I? They'll be speaking in Spanish.'

'Oh yeah.'

Lee and Will plonked themselves onto a sofa near the manager's office doorway. The swirly green, red and white covers were slippy and their sweaty legs stuck to them.

'But you can tell loads from the way people speak, or the way they act, so we might be able to work out what they're up to.'

'You think they're up to something they shouldn't be?'

'What do you think?'

'Well, from past experience I'd say that you've got a great imagination …'

'So …?'

'So don't let it run away with you. It's probably nothing. They could just be friends or brothers. Or maybe the guy in the shiny suit owns this place.'

'Don't look now,' Lee said, 'but here comes your guy.'

Will looked, of course, but the younger shiny-suited man ignored him as he strode confidently past the reception desk and over to the manager's office, which he entered without bothering to knock.

'He certainly acts like he owns the place,' Lee said.

The door was closed gently, the way a burglar might close it if worried about being heard.

'Do you need the toilet?' Will asked, nodding at the Gents near the reception desk.

Lee cottoned on immediately. 'Oh, right, yes, I've never been more desperate.'

'Well you go in first and I'll wait for you.'

Lee bounced up from the sofa and headed for the lavatories. Will followed, coming to a halt right outside the door of the manager's office.

'I won't be long,' Lee called back.

'Take your time,' Will told him more loudly than was strictly necessary, just as an attractive girl their age was passing. 'It's bad for your bowels if you push too hard.'

The girl stared at Lee with a 'Too Much Information' face. Lee glared at Will. He was all for keeping things realistic, but that was over the top.

The Gents was horrible. A roll of toilet paper had sneaked out of the single cubicle and had attempted to reach the wash basin, only to be cut off in its prime by a soaking that had stuck its entrails to the floor. And to think that some people might be in their bare feet when they needed the toilet. Yuck!

Now that Lee was in the Gents there was the question of what he should actually do. What if someone came in? It would seem rather odd if he was found hovering outside the cubicle as if listening to people doing their business. No, that would be too weird, so he entered the cubicle. At least if he was inside it no one would be suspicious. Not that he was actually doing anything suspicious anyway – he was actually trying to do good – but sometimes when you were trying to act normal it made you feel as if you were up to something. It was the same in shops; if you saw a security guard you tried to look totally innocent, but always felt as if someone might have filled your bag with stolen goods.

Once inside the cubicle, Lee realised that he couldn't just stand any old way. Someone coming in would be able to see his feet under the gap around the sides. He needed to either face towards the toilet or face away from it. He chose to face away to give himself the option of sitting down and to avoid having to stand for a while without making a peeing noise.

As he had entered the cubicle, the cistern had been filling up noisily, a sure sign that someone had not long left. As the water in the cistern reached its maximum level, it brought voices rather than the total silence Lee had been expecting.

Lee quickly ruled out the possibility that this meant he was going mad (though those who knew him well might not have been quite so hasty). He also ruled out the possibility that there were other people in the Gents because he had only just entered. But then … where were the voices coming from?

He nervously lifted the lid on the toilet – just in case there was actually someone in there. Nothing. He stood still again and … and yes, it really was as if the voices were coming from the ceiling.

In fact, they were coming through the vent at the

top of the wall. And, now that Lee thought about it, he realised that wall ran down the side of the manager's office, meaning these had to be voices from inside that room.

Bingo! It was the hotel manager and the men in shiny suits!

The vent was high up on the wall, but Lee wasn't going to let that stop him. By standing on the flimsy plastic seat and grabbing the toilet door with one hand he was able to lean over just far enough to get his ear to the vent. He was careful not to let his ear touch the vent because it had clearly not been cleaned since the hotel had been built and was even hairier than his granny's chin, which was saying something. Still, being that close made all the difference. Although he couldn't hear everything, he could hear the voices clearly enough that he could make out a few phrases, especially as, to his surprise, all three men were speaking in English, not Spanish.

'… need to be careful. Not too many times …' This man spoke quickly and with a strong Spanish accent.

'I say as many as we can get away with.' Another Spanish accent but the voice deeper and calmer.

And then an English accent, or maybe it was Welsh. Or maybe even Irish. Lee wasn't very good at telling one accent from another. 'This is our best route in, so we need to protect it. But we also need to work it – make it pay its way.'

The first man again. 'I realise that, but we can't take too many chances. None of us can afford to get caught.'

'Especially you,' the calm voice pointed out without much sympathy.

There was a brief silence before the English/Welsh/Irish voice spoke again. 'When is the next shipment due?'

'Friday evening,' Calm Voice replied.

'And you wanna use the same room?' The quick-speaking Spaniard was becoming a little panicky. 'But the hotel is always really busy then, the …'

And then there was another voice. One from inside the Gents. 'Lee!'

'Wha …' Lee got such a fright that his hand slipped on the toilet door and he fell off the seat. His bum slid down the side of the cubicle until it reached the wet floor.

'Lee?' It was Will. 'Are you okay?'

'Oh man, this floor is … Look at my shorts! Everyone will think I've wet myself!'

Lee picked himself off the tiled floor. Only his pride was hurt, but pride could take longer to heal than a broken limb.

'I didn't mean to give you a fright. It was just that you were taking quite a while and it didn't feel right hanging about outside that door.'

'Shhh,' Lee told him.

'What?' Will looked behind him. 'Why?'

'They might hear you.'

'Who might?'

Lee opened the cubicle door and stepped out, just as the hotel manager stepped in.

'Is everything okay?' he asked, doing a poor job of hiding his irritation. 'I heard banging, like someone was falling or … What happened to your shorts? Did you …?'

'No, I didn't,' Lee made clear. 'I sat on a wet patch.'

'On the toilet? But surely you pulled your shorts down before …'

'Outside, at the side of the pool, before I came in.'

'Well it will soon dry. You are okay though?'

'Yes, thanks. I just slipped.'

'The floor, it is all wet. I will get a cleaner to come in

a minute. But right now I am in a meeting.'

'Yes, I know …,' slipped out of Lee's mouth before he could stop it, so he added, '… you have a very responsible job,' which got him off the hook.

The manager nodded and exited the Gents.

'That was close,' Lee whispered.

'Was it?'

Lee waved Will over to the cubicle and pointed to the vent. 'Climb up and have a listen while I keep watch outside. But don't make any loud noises.'

'Who is it?'

'It's them.'

Will understood, so Lee left him to it. He was halfway out of the Gents when he remembered the big wet patch on his shorts, so he kept his back against the wall and tried to rub off some of the water onto the front of a plastic sign, but that made his bum even wetter. He would have to hold on and use the electric dryer.

Lee stuck his head back round the corner of the Gents. 'Can you hear anything?' he asked.

'Shhh,' Will replied, from which Lee took it that his best friend was listening intently.

It seemed an age before Will reappeared. When he did he was in a hurry. 'They're coming out,' he said urgently and motioned Lee away from the Gents, across the reception area, back towards the pool table. Lee waited until they were almost out of sight before casting a glance over his shoulder. Sure enough, the two shiny suits were leaving the manager's office.

And also sure enough, several adults and children were pointing at the big wet patch at the back of Lee's shorts.

As the pool table was off to one side, away from everyone else, it was a good place to talk. The couple who had been at the table had left, leaving it to Lee and Will.

'What do you think it all means?' Will asked. 'What's going on?'

'Tell me again what you heard,' Lee said as he tried to pot a striped pool ball. He sent the cue forward but caught the bottom edge of the white ball, making it jump into the air and over the ball he was trying to hit.

'One of them …'

'Which one?'

'The Welsh one.'

'Ah, so you think he's Welsh too. Okay.'

'Anyway, he said he needed to get things to Cardiff by the end of next week.'

'What things?'

'I don't know.'

'What else did they say?'

'If you stop interrupting I'll be able to tell you.'

'They said that?'

'No, you keep …'

'Aw. Sorry.'

'One of them also said …'

'Which one?'

'The Spanish one with the deep voice. Not the manager, the other one. He said that timescale should be possible. Then the manager said he didn't want any traces left. He wanted it to be as if no one had ever been in the room.'

'Which room?'

'They didn't say.'

'Pity.' Lee nodded at the table. 'It's your turn.'

Will at least managed to hit the ball he was aiming for. It rolled over a pocket, leaving Will an easy shot for later in the game. As he stood up he continued. 'I think the manager was worried about the other two men being there.'

'Maybe he thought the reflection off their shiny suits might damage his eyes.'

Will chortled, then said seriously, 'I don't think he wants to go along with their plans, but he has to. He said he wanted this to be the last time, but the other Spanish guy just laughed in quite a scary way and then said something in Spanish that I didn't understand.'

'Because it was in Spanish, I'd guess.'

'Yeah. Maybe we could ask your mum to translate.'

'Can you remember what it was he said?'

'Actually … no.'

'Don't worry, she'd probably get it completely wrong anyway. He could be saying "Don't mess with me" and she'd probably say it was, "What's your favourite kind of pizza?"'

Lee finally potted a ball. Unfortunately it was one of Will's.

'Two shots to me,' Will stated and proceeded to pot three balls in a row. 'Do you think we should tell someone?' he asked as he straightened from his last shot.

'Who would we tell?'

'Your dad?'

'No.'

'Your mum?'

'No.'

'The police?'

'No.'

'Lee …'

'Oops, sorry, I was doing that 'no' thing again, wasn't I?'

'Yes, you were.' Will handed him the cue. 'Your shot.'

Lee lined up an easy pot and sank it. He lined up another and again the ball slipped into the pocket. He was on a roll.

'The thing is,' he said, looking up, 'what would we say? We don't know what, if anything, is really happening, so what could Mum or Dad do?'

Another striped ball was sitting over a corner pocket. Lee bent down, lined up the shot and … balls scattered everywhere, sending the black ball into one of the middle pockets.

'Hah!' Will cried. 'I win!'

'How did I miss that?' Lee asked himself.

Game over, they headed back to the pool.

'All we can do is keep an eye out for anything strange going on,' Lee said.

'Maybe we could follow the manager,' Will suggested. 'Or the guys in shiny suits.'

'Yeah, maybe we should. But let's get some lunch first. I'm starving.'

It was a lot busier at the poolside than when they had left. And something was missing, Lee noticed as he went to sit down.

'Hey, where's my sunlounger?'

Will was also looking around for his. 'What's going on?'

Lee's mum lowered her book and sat up. 'Oh, you're back at last.'

'We were just playing pool,' Lee told her.

'Right. Well I'm afraid that your sunloungers have been requisitioned.'

'Eh … what does that mean?'

'It means they were taken by the management.'

'Taken where?'

'To be given to someone else.'

'But I was going to use it again. It had my towel on

it.'

'Oh don't worry, I've salvaged your towel.'

'Bad luck,' Will mumbled.

Lee looked around but it was impossible to tell which sunlounger had been his; they all looked the same.

'Who did they give it to?' he asked.

'Those people over there.' His mum nodded to the far corner of the pool (it being rude to point, of course), where a family was arranging their sunloungers so that they pointed directly at the sun. They were lining them up with some precision. Lee suspected they might even be using protractors to ensure they achieved exactly the right angle.

'No way. Not *them*. Not the toffs from the plane.'

'I'm afraid so. They claimed that they had paid for a higher grade of holiday package, one that allows them to have a sunlounger whenever they want it.'

'What! Even if someone else is already using it?'

'So it would seem.'

'But that's not fair. We've paid for our holiday too.'

'My point exactly,' Lee's dad said, knocking his book off his face, where it had been acting as a sunshade. 'I told the manager it was outrageous.'

'It can't have been the manager,' Lee said. 'We saw him … inside.' He realised he was on dodgy ground, in danger of revealing what he and Will had been up to.

'The deputy manager, then. Whoever it was that came out and said that bunch over there were to have them because it said in the small print of their holiday contract, blah blah blah …'

'Didn't you try to stop him?'

'Your dad's already managed to throw one member of staff in the swimming pool,' Lee's mum said. 'Probably best that he doesn't throw the deputy manager in as well.'

'That was an accident,' Lee's dad protested. 'My

book flew up and …'

'Anyway,' Lee's mum continued, 'it was better not to kick up a stink around the pool and spoil everyone's holidays.'

'But what about *our* holiday,' Lee argued. 'Will and I have nowhere to sit now. Do they expect us to stand the whole time we're here?'

'You'll be in the pool most of the time, won't you?'

Lee remembered what was in the pool courtesy of Rebecca. 'Eh, no, I was planning to read a bit and … have a sleep.'

'Really? That's most unlike you. Sleeping during the day …'

'Must be the travelling,' Lee's dad decided. 'And maybe the chlorine in the pool.'

'Yes,' Lee agreed. 'Something like that.'

'Here, you can share my sunlounger,' Lee's dad offered. 'I've had enough of lying around for now. I want to see a bit of the resort.' He stood and stretched. 'I take it none of you want to come along?' he asked once his arms were back in their normal positions.

He was correct. The others all wanted to stay where they were.

'Trust you to be getting restless already,' Lee's mum told him. 'We're barely here five minutes and you're off on your wanders.'

'Well we've come all this way, so we might as well see a bit of the place. Are you sure no one wants to come along?'

Lee, his mum, Will and Rebecca all shook their heads.

'Oh well, I'll go on my lonesome then,' Lee's dad declared and, after pulling on a shirt, he set off towards the main road.

Lee and Will were sitting in the middle of the sun-lounger Lee's dad had vacated.

'I can't believe it,' Lee said.

'Neither can I,' Will agreed.

'But you don't know what I'm talking about.'

'That's true. But I'm agreeing with you anyway.'

'Aw.'

'So what is it that you can't believe?'

'That The Perfects are not only in the same resort as us, they're in the same hotel! Just our luck.'

'They weren't down here yesterday,' Will pointed out. 'I wonder why not.'

'Maybe their butler mislaid their swimming trunks and they had to get their chauffeur to drive for miles in their Rolls Royce so they could find a shop that sold replacements of a suitably high quality.'

'Or maybe they were up in their room pigging out on a special delivery of Belgian chocs.'

'Jolly spiffing, Old Boy.'

'I'm surprised they're slumming it here,' Will said.

Lee was offended. 'This place isn't *that* bad. The odd cockroach infestation perhaps …'

'No, no, I didn't mean it like that. Just that you'd think they'd be in a mansion somewhere, with lots of servants running after them.'

'Yeah. I'm amazed they're prepared to share the same pool as us commoners.'

'They're not actually in the pool yet,' Will noted.

'Probably too concerned that their hair will get all out of shape and won't look quite right for the opera tonight. I mean, what would people think if their hair looked slightly frizzy, or if a strand stuck up!'

'I think they'd say that it would be in keeping with their stuck up noses.'

Perfect Son was casting a wary eye at the swimming pool, as if fearful that it might cause him to get wet.

There was a girl beside him who had to be his sister. There were distinct family likenesses; Perfect Son and Perfect Father were both slightly chubby (too many Belgian chocs) and walked as if they needed to find a toilet in a hurry; Perfect Mother and Perfect Daughter both had faces carved with a blunt chisel and walked like ballet dancers, trying to float along on tiny wings created by their hands sticking out at the sides.

'They look like a right bundle of laughs,' Will commented.

'About as funny as a school test, I'd say. I hate them.'

Will turned and looked at Lee. 'Why?' he asked. 'Why do you hate them? Because they're loaded?'

Lee shook his head. 'No. Why should I care how much money they've got? If I hated them because of that, other people would be able to hate me just because my family is richer than theirs. I'll bet there are loads of people who are really rich but also really nice. You shouldn't have to be one or the other.'

'That's true …'

'So no, it's not their money, it's their attitude. It stinks. It wouldn't matter how much money I had, I still wouldn't make someone give up their sunlounger for me.'

Will held his hand up to keep the sun from his eyes. 'I'm roasting,' he complained. 'I think I'm going to melt.'

'It's the middle of the day. The sun's at it's highest, which means it's nearest our part of Earth and doesn't have so much atmosphere to get through to get to us.'

'Crikey, how come you know all that?'

'The Ogre told us.'

'I thought you couldn't stand her.'

'I suppose she's alright sometimes. Some of the stuff she tells us is quite interesting.'

'When she's not breathing fire, you mean.'

'Exactly. She only told us that because she came in one day as red as tomato sauce and had to explain why.'

'I take it she'd been out in the sun.'

'Yes, and she'd fallen asleep and burnt her arms and legs.'

'You sure it wasn't just that she breathed on herself by mistake?'

'Good point. It could have been,' Lee said.

Will placed a shirt over his head.

'Better?' Lee asked.

'Not much.' He returned the shirt to the end of the sunlounger. 'Come on, let's go swimming to cool off.'

'Eh ….'

But Will had already made up his mind and jumped into the pool before Lee could say, *Don't go in there! Rebecca peed in it earlier!* As it was, Will seemed not to be suffering any ill effects when he surfaced. 'Is it okay?' Lee called.

'It's brilliant,' Will told him. 'So much cooler.'

'Are you sure it doesn't smell funny or taste strange?'

'Eh? Why should it?'

Lee decided to risk it. Hopefully the hotel had installed a powerful filter in the pool, one that strained off anything … undesirable that might be in the pool. Nonetheless, he kept his mouth firmly closed as he swam.

Will, not usually an instigator of pranks, decided that the Perfect Family should get wet. He led Lee round the side of the pool to the point where the family had established themselves. There they both held on to the pool ledge, stretched their legs out behind them and kicked the water as hard as they could, sending sploshes high above and around them.

There was a commotion above them, but out of

sight. 'Hoy! What do you think you're playing at?' a man called. Seconds later an immaculately groomed head loomed over the side. It was Perfect Father. 'I say,' the man blustered. 'What's going on here?'

Will played dumb. 'Pardon? We were just practising our swimming stroke, like our instructor told us to.'

'Yeah, that's right,' Lee agreed, thinking that it was unlike Will to have a laugh at someone else's expense; that was normally his own job.

'Well I didn't pay good money to come here and have my family soaked by the likes of you. It's most inconsiderate. Please desist at once.'

'Okay,' Will said brightly, and he and Will swam across the pool on their backs, watching as Perfect Father sat back down on his sunlounger and put a flat cap on his head.

'What's with the cap?' Lee said to Will.

'No idea. Probably thinks it's rude to be seen in public without a hat.'

'He looks like he should be out in the country in one of those ancient cars with no roofs.'

'Maybe flat caps are all the rage where he lives.'

Splashing the Perfect Family had been fun, so they decided to think up some more pranks they could play on them over the remainder of the week.

Almost two hours passed before Lee's dad reappeared.

'Where have you been?' Lee's mum immediately began interrogating him. 'Off helping that rep dry the clothes you soaked?'

Lee's dad waved his hand. 'Oh you know; here, there and everywhere.'

Lee's mum knew his dad too well. 'You've been up to

something, haven't you? I can tell.'

'Well, I've booked a car for tomorrow so we can get around and see the place.'

'Oh. Well that's okay, I suppose.'

'And, guess what else?'

'What?' Lee, Will, Rebecca and Lee's mum all asked, since none of them knew.

'I bumped into someone we know!'

'Really!' Lee's mum was amazed. 'Who?'

A large hand placed itself on Lee's mum's shoulder and a voice behind her said, 'Me!'

They all turned around, and there before them, in the loudest shorts and T-shirt they had ever seen – the sort that ought to be banned by the style police – was Lee's Uncle Raymond – his mum's brother.

Lee's mum jumped up, delighted, if shocked, to see him. 'What on earth are you doing here?'

'Uncle Raymond, Uncle Raymond!' Rebecca chanted, urging him to pick her up.

'Bit of a surprise?' Lee's dad asked them all.

'You bet,' they all said together as if they'd been rehearsing.

Lee's mum looked around. 'Where's Liz?' she asked, referring to Raymond's partner.

'Oh she's back at home looking after the guests at the bed and breakfast. She doesn't much like the sun anyway.'

'So why are *you* here?'

'I thought I'd surprise you.' He winked. 'A certain person was in on it all. A certain person standing not too far from me.' He clapped Lee's dad on the back.

'So is that why you disappeared off?' Lee's mum asked.

'Amongst other reasons.'

Lee's mum put her arms around her brother's neck. Lee and Will turned away whilst she kissed him on the cheek. 'This is fantastic!'

'Well I'm glad you're glad I'm here.'

Lee was glad, too. Uncle Raymond was a great laugh. He would happily encourage Lee to do all the things his mum and dad normally said he shouldn't. In fact, Lee wondered just how happy his mum was to see her brother, because it wasn't all that long ago that Lee had overheard her telling him off for making it difficult to keep Lee on the straight and narrow. 'You egg him on something rotten,' she'd said.

However, they must have patched things up, as families should do, because otherwise he wouldn't be there. Now this could be a *really* good holiday, Lee decided.

That evening it was Lee's mum and dad's choice as to where to eat.

'We're going to have tapas,' Lee's dad announced.

'What! No way! I'm starving! I can't go without food until morning!'

'No, no, you're misunderstanding me. Tapas is a traditional style of Spanish food with loads of different bits and pieces. You stick them all in the middle of the table and then help yourself to whichever bits you fancy. There's bound to be something you'll all like.'

'I promise you, it's delicious,' Uncle Raymond assured a sceptical Lee, Will and Rebecca. 'Just you wait.'

Off they set, with Uncle Raymond carrying Rebecca on his shoulders. Lee would have asked for a go, too, except he thought maybe that wasn't cool at his age and people might laugh at him.

Carrying Rebecca all that way was easy for Uncle Raymond because he was a strong man. Not the sort of strong man who can pull trains along with his teeth or bend railway track between his toes; rather, the sort who is strong in a healthy, robust, without-having-tried-too-hard way. That was because he was a farmer and, unlike Lee's dad, didn't sit at a desk all day but was instead out in the fields much of the time lifting, pushing and carrying.

'How's your farm,' Will asked as they walked.

'It's fine, thank you, Young Man. You should come over to it one day.'

'I'd love to,' Will enthused. 'That would be brilliant.'

'You're welcome any time Lee's coming to see us. There aren't any cows to milk or sheep to sheer, mind. It's only arable farming that we do – crops and the like.'

'I don't care. I've never been on a farm.'

'Ever?'

'Never ever.'

'Well don't leave it too long, then.'

They were almost there, Lee's dad assured them when Rebecca asked.

'When and where did you get your gear?' Lee's mum asked Uncle Raymond.

'The clothes? Why, d'you like them?'

'Eh, well they're … bright.'

Uncle Raymond was still wearing the same garish shirt and shorts he'd arrived in. The shorts were fluorescent green and the shirt had so many colours in it that even one of those amazing colour-changing chameleons would have had trouble camouflaging itself against it.

'I thought you might remember these. I've had them for years. Since not long after I left school, in fact.'

'Is that right. I'd never have guessed …'

'Yeah, I'm surprised I can still fit into them.'

In truth he barely could. The shirt was tight over his chest, and as for the trousers, let's just say it would be best if he didn't sit down in a hurry.

They reached the restaurant and were shown to a big round table. Lee's dad was pleased to find that the waiters were less smarmy than in the previous evening's establishment, and also more efficient. The menus were down in front of them almost as soon as they'd sat down, closely followed by some wine.

'Right, let's have a look and see what we have on offer,' Lee's dad said. He was eager to get stuck in, having told them for the last two hours just how much he loved tapas.

'Why don't you just order a load of stuff,' Lee's mum suggested, and then we can all help ourselves to whatever looks appetising.'

'Good idea,' everyone agreed and left Lee's dad to it.

It was fifteen minutes before the first of the dishes arrived.

'Patatas bravas,' the waiter announced as he lowered a plate of potatoes in a reddy-brown sauce.

'Ah, potatoes that put up a brave fight before being harvested,' Uncle Raymond suggested.

'Just be careful, because sometimes that sauce can be quite firey,' Lee's dad warned.

'Ensalada Cau Ferrat,' was next to be announced.

'The lid of a ferret,' Uncle Raymond translated, not very well because it was salad that was placed in front of them.

'Tortilla Español.'

Lee's mum thought she'd better contribute to the translating, and for once got it right. 'That's Spanish omelette.'

As they began to share what was in front of them, yet more food arrived and they gave up trying to translate everything and settled for eating it instead.

Lee wasn't too sure about some of it. Calamari, his mum explained, was fried squid. Lee had seen a squid on TV. It was a bit like a jellyfish. 'What does it taste like?' he asked.

'Squash balls,' Uncle Raymond answered. 'It's delicious.'

Lee was even less convinced than before.

'Can you pass the meatballs?' Uncle Raymond asked Lee's mum.

'What's the magic word?' Lee's mum asked back, treating him like a child.

'Quickly,' Uncle Raymond said.

This was the sort of thing Uncle Raymond was always coming out with. Lee's mum frowned as she passed them over. 'Just remember that that's a joke,' she warned Lee and Will and Rebecca. 'That's not what you normally say.'

'That's right,' Uncle Raymond said sternly. 'You're in Spain, so it's 'pronto' instead of 'quickly'.'

'You're such a bad influence,' Lee's mum told her brother.

'Bring me an omelette pronto!' Rebecca playfully demanded of a passing waiter, before her dad explained that she was just over-excited.

Lee's mum could see all her good work on her youngest child's manners coming undone.

'Well,' Uncle Raymond said. 'Here's to happy holidays!' Everyone picked up their glass and raised it to the middle of the table where they clinked it off everyone else's glass in a toast.

As the glasses were returned to the table Uncle Raymond let out a long and very loud burp. 'Oh my goodness,' he said. 'This beer's gassy.'

'Raymond!' Lee's mum said. 'Come on, stop it now. Everyone's looking at us.'

They all looked around, and right enough a few old biddies and the likes were tutting away. 'Pardon me,' Uncle Raymond said to those nearest to them. 'It's this

Spanish water. It's full of bubbles.'

Uncle Raymond seemed to take the hint from Lee's mum's hard stare and behaved himself after that.

'So what are we doing tomorrow?' Lee asked as the meal ended and after his mum had insisted that he couldn't ask for the bill 'pronto'.

'Going out in the car to find us some countryside,' his dad said.

'I was hoping we could go to a water park or somewhere like that.'

'Well we can do that another day. It's the countryside tomorrow.'

'That'll be great,' Uncle Raymond said. 'What with working on a farm, I hardly ever get to see any countryside. It'll be quite a novelty.'

DAY TWO

'Is that it!' Lee's mum couldn't believe her eyes as she stepped outside the front door of the hotel. 'I know I said to try and get a bargain, but …' She ran out of words.

She was staring at the car her husband had hired. It was … basic. Well, actually, that would be too flattering. It was tiny, old and, so far as any of them could see, made from paper held together – though only very loosely – by sticky tape. It appeared that it might once have been red, but they couldn't be certain.

'It wasn't quite what I had in mind,' Lee's dad admitted.

'Why didn't you insist on something better?'

'It's peak season. All their other cars have been rented out. I know it's not perfect, but at least it goes.'

Uncle Raymond was shaking his head. 'My tractor could outrun that heap of …'

'Not in front of the children,' Lee's mum interrupted. 'Rebecca's still young and impressionable.'

'Whereas Lee's beyond salvation,' Lee's dad contributed.

'I was only going to say horse manure,' Uncle Raymond said, defending his reputation. 'That car's a load of horse manure. What's wrong with that?'

Judging from Lee's mum's face, she clearly didn't believe him, but let it go anyway.

'How are we all going to fit inside?' Lee's mum asked. 'I suppose I'll have to squeeze in the back with the kids. There's no way Raymond will fit in with them, not unless he sticks his legs out of the sunroof.'

Uncle Raymond seemed to think that might be fun, until he realised there was no sunroof to stick his legs out of.

'It's only for one day,' Lee's dad tried to reassure them. 'We'll manage.'

'What about seat belts?'

Lee's dad looked into the car. 'Yep, it's got those,' he said.

'We'll head out into the countryside, then up into the mountains to see some of the villages there,' Lee's dad said, 'where we can stop so we can all get out of the car and stretch our legs.'

'Sounds fascinating,' Lee said sarcastically.

'You'll love it!' his dad enthused. 'Wait 'til you're up there and see them. They're very traditional and authentic.' Lee's dad was beginning to sound like the holiday reps. 'And I think I've found us a vineyard we can visit on the way back.'

Uncle Raymond's ears pricked up at that idea. He liked his wine. 'Hey, now you're talking.'

It took five minutes for them to pack themselves into the car. 'Dad, could you not have got a horse and cart,' Lee moaned. 'It would have been more comfortable.'

'And faster,' Uncle Raymond added.

'Music!' Rebecca commanded.

Her dad reached down to switch on the radio … except there wasn't one. 'Eh, sorry to disappoint you, Rebecca, but I believe that was an optional extra that I didn't pay for,' he said.

Rebecca had absolutely no idea what he was talking about.

'Tell you what, Rebecca,' Uncle Raymond said, 'we'll make our own music, will we?'

'Yeah!' Rebecca cried. She had never heard Uncle Raymond sing before. But then few people had, or few that were alive to tell the tale, it was so bad. Legend had it (i.e. Lee's dad had made up the story and told it to Lee) that three of Uncle Raymond's friends had been with him in his car one night when Uncle Raymond had started to sing. His singing was so bad that the three friends had opened the car doors and, in desperation, had flung themselves upon the mercies of the road and other traffic rather than have to spend a second longer being acoustically accosted. Unfortunately, it had been a deeply dark night and they hadn't realised they were crossing a very low-sided bridge at the time, and all three had landed in the river below. They had been swept off to sea and it was said that, after clinging for days to a log, all three had been washed up in Madagascar, off the south-east coast of Africa, where they had established a small fish and chip shop to try to earn their fare home. That had been eleven years ago, so presumably fish and chips weren't too popular with the Madagascans.

'*I could be so lucky; lucky, lucky, lucky; lucky, lucky, lucky, lucky-y-y,*' Uncle Raymond howled.

Will looked at Lee and laughed. 'No,' Lee said. 'Believe it or not, that's him trying his hardest. He's completely tone deaf.'

'That's not right,' Rebecca said, and sang her own version, which, though by no means perfect, was certainly a lot easier on the ears.

It had been a few years since Lee's dad had driven abroad and it was taking a bit of getting used to. The steering wheel was on the opposite side from the one at home, and everyone was driving on the other side of the road. At roundabouts you had to be careful to look left instead of right and then go round anti-clockwise. It felt so weird at first, but they soon grew used to it. Anyway, there were other distractions to occupy them; like the window winder that fell off when Uncle

Raymond tried to turn it; like the way your bum felt every single bump in the road; and like the rearview mirror that fell off the front windscreen when Lee's dad tried to adjust it.

'This is, without doubt, the worst car I've ever been in,' Lee's mum stated. No one disagreed with her.

Undaunted by the reaction to his last attempt at a song, Uncle Raymond tried again. '*I see a little silhouetto of a man …*'

'Where?' Rebecca asked, looking around.

'*Scaramouch, scaramouch, will you do the Flamenco …?*'

'*Fandango*,' Lee's dad corrected. '*Will you do the* Fandango?'

'We're in Spain!' Uncle Raymond cried. 'It's the Spanish version.' They were passing an old church now. '*Spare him his life from this monastery …*'

They reached a road junction where Lee's dad was convinced he had right of way and began to pull out, expecting another car to stop for them. It didn't. Lee's dad had to jump hard on the brakes and, after a delay that seemed like several weeks, they kicked in and slowed the car. Lee's dad was fuming. 'The stupid …'

'*Bismillah! No – he would not let you go,*' Uncle Raymond croaked, just in time to save Lee's dad from lapsing into swearing.

'*Let him go!*' Lee and Will sang together.

'*Bismillah! No – they will not let him go.*'

'*Let him go!*'

'*Bismillah! No – they will not let him go. Will not let him go. Oh let him go, go, go, go …*'

'*No, no, no, no, no, no …*'

'Yes, that's us.' Lee's dad was finally able to ease out into the traffic and the song was ended, much to the relief of Lee's mum.

The mountains were dramatic, rising up behind the

resort. The roads were equally dramatic, with tight bends and steep ascents. On one occasion Lee's dad had to exhort them all to pedal hard, even though there weren't any pedals, because it seemed that the little clapped-out car wasn't going to make it. (He didn't repeat the request for fear that their feet would go through the car's floor.) However, it held out, albeit just, and they reached the village they were aiming for shortly after midday.

The place was deserted. The locals all had more sense than to be outside in the sun at that time of day. 'They must all be off having their siestas,' Lee's dad decided.

The village was as old as the hills it stood on. Most of the stone buildings were in good condition, although a few were, like one of Lee's grannies, beginning to show their age. 'Can you imagine living here?' Lee's mum said, admiring the view out across the sea.

'No,' Lee said. 'There's nothing to do. I'd be bored out of my mind.'

Will agreed. 'No wonder they're all off having siestas. Sleeping's probably the most exciting thing that ever happens here.'

They walked to the middle of the village, where a small fountain with a small font stood amongst equally small trees. This was it, the highlight of the village tour; a fountain that, if it was anywhere else, you would walk past without even noticing.

A few old men sat under an awning that protruded over the pavement from a café bar. This was what passed for having a social life in these places, Lee realised – falling asleep over a coffee or a beer, or watching the world go by, which didn't take much concentration because very little of it ever did go by; just a few tourists, who were desperate to get out of their holiday resorts and stumbled into this separate world.

'It's like going back in time,' Lee said.

'I'm sure a lot of the people who live here now have been here all their lives,' his dad remarked.

Your whole life in a place like this! Where Lee lived would never seem too bad ever again. Home was like a giant theme park compared to an armpit like this.

And yet his mum and dad and Uncle Raymond all seemed to find something to like about it. 'Isn't it quaint,' his mum said, while his dad commented, 'I'd love to see inside one of the houses. I'm sure it would be fascinating. So olde worlde.'

Uncle Raymond had also found something he liked. 'It has a bar. That's good enough for me.'

They'd been there for all of ten minutes when Lee said, 'Right, is that us? We've seen everything there is to see – twice.' He was desperate to get back to the hotel. The dodgy geezers in shiny suits could be up to anything, and he and Will ought to be keeping an eye on them.

'Just be patient,' his mum chastised. 'We're enjoying this.'

'What is there to enjoy, Mum?'

'The peace and tranquillity. This place is so relaxing. Or it is when you're not buzzing like a mosquito about getting out of here.'

An ancient woman dressed entirely in black shuffled past them, and Lee's mum got all excited. 'Oh look! Someone in traditional dress!'

It might have been traditional, but Lee could see why it wasn't popular.

'She could be in mourning,' Lee's dad explained. 'Maybe her husband's died.'

'Or her dog,' Rebecca suggested, 'because she hasn't got one with her.'

'Rebecca,' Lee said. 'Most of the people we've met don't have dogs with them, but that doesn't mean their dogs have died.'

They wandered up a couple of side-streets and Lee's parents admired yet more old buildings. Then, having walked every metre of road in less than twenty minutes, they all returned to the square and took a seat on the benches that were shaded by the tree.

'Ah, isn't this a lovely spot,' Lee's mum sighed.

She certainly thought so. So did a bird that had perched above them amongst the tree's dark-green leaves. It was a perfect spot – the fountain nearby, the café bar from which to scavenge lose crumbs from bread and cakes, and some tourists' heads on which to drop horrible, acidic, white poo.

It chose Uncle Raymond as its target, perhaps because he had the biggest head, making it easier to hit. 'Oh man!' He leapt up. 'What the …?' He put his hand to his head then brought it back down and looked at it. Not a pretty sight. 'That's all I need. Where is the little sod?' He searched the tree above. Lee couldn't remember if Uncle Raymond had a shotgun for his farm, but reckoned that for the bird's sake it was as well that, if he did own one, he didn't have it with him now.

Everyone tried very hard not to laugh as Uncle Raymond used the fountain to wash the gunge off his head. As he did so, a local came across to them. He said something flamboyant in Spanish that none of them, including Lee's mum, could understand. 'Que?' she said. 'No entiendo.'

The Spaniard realised they spoke English and, pointing at Uncle Raymond's head, said, 'The birds, yes? That why we no sit here.'

They got the general idea.

Uncle Raymond decided that they should visit the café bar after that little episode.

Lee's mum couldn't argue with that in the circumstances and so they headed off, especially after Uncle Raymond said he'd treat them all to lunch.

After they'd paid up they set off back down the mountain. There were a few scary moments when the car's brakes didn't seem too keen to stop it, but they made it down in one piece.

Everyone was tired by the time they reached the hotel, so it was decided that a power nap was in order before they headed out to eat.

Lee conked out instantly, but his sleep wasn't restful. He dreamed of the Shiny Suits and the hotel manager and what they might be up to. Will was in his dream, saying, 'Lee, quick! You've got to see this!'

And then he was being rocked from side to side.

'See what?' Lee said.

'Hurry! Open your eyes!'

'I can't, this is a dream. You're not real. I'm just imagining you.'

The rocking grew stronger. It was more like a violent shake.

'Lee!' Will whispered loudly.

'I can't save the world just yet … I'm sleeping.'

'No, you're very much awake but you're talking like a loony.'

'Eh?' Lee sprung up. 'What?'

'Come on!' Will insisted and dragged Lee to the window, where he pointed at something below.

Lee rubbed the sleep from his eyes. 'What am I supposed to be looking for …?'

But there was no need for Will to answer. The sleek, shiny open-top car sitting outside the hotel's main entrance spoke for itself.

'Wow! A Rolls Royce!'

'Yeah, I know. And look who's inside it.'

Lee had been too dazzled by the car's exterior to bother looking inside it.

'A chauffeur!'

'Yes, yes, but never mind him.'

'Why not? It's pretty impressive to have a chauffeur.'

'But look who's in the back.'

Lee took a closer look. The sun was quite low in the sky and he had to squint to see clearly. Or maybe he needed to ask his mum and dad to take him to get his eyes checked. Perhaps he needed glasses. If so, hopefully he would be allowed those dark wrap-around ones that pop stars wore so he could look really cool, even if no one would speak to him because they wouldn't be able to see his eyes.

'Oh man! No way!' he exclaimed, returning his concentration to who was inside the car. 'It can't be.'

'It is,' Will pointed out.

'But it can't be.'

'Why not?'

'It just can't. Not them again. Not The Perfect Family!'

'You were right all along. It's exactly as you said. They've made their chauffeur drive all the way here so he can take them wherever they need to go.'

Mrs Perfect was wearing a pale green evening dress and a necklace that obviously contained loads of diamonds because the sun was reflecting off them and dazzling Lee. She was also wearing a dead vulture on her head. Or at least that's what her hat looked like. Mr Perfect had, for once, discarded his flat cap but had replaced it with a boater – a straw sun hat. He had also swapped his pool gear for a blazer, shirt and tie. Perfect Son and Perfect Daughter were similarly well groomed, ready to be shown off to the bigwigs of high society.

'Where do you think they get all their money from?' Will said.

'Maybe they're a crime gang,' Will suggested.

'Yeah, like the Mafia.'

'Although they're too posh to be criminals.'

'You get posh criminals.'

'Maybe they won the lottery.'

'Hmm. No, I reckon they've always had loads of money. Listen to the way they speak and the way they take everything for granted. They've never had to do without.'

'Yeah, and I'll bet their tent's never been flooded out,' Lee added. 'Because they wouldn't know what a tent looks like.'

As they pondered the source of the Perfect Family's great wealth, another flashy car pulled up behind. A red sports car.

'A Ferrari!' Will pointed out immediately. He had always been better than Lee at recognising makes of cars, mainly because his dad was interested in them and had taught him which kind was which. Will's dad was desperate to get a fast car, but Will's mum wasn't interested. She said that cars gave everyone asthma, killed animals and made people lazy. Everyone should be forced to ride bikes everywhere, she reckoned, even though she didn't own one herself and drove everywhere she went.

A tall, tanned man in a dark suit slid out of the gleaming Ferrari.

'They must have a Rolls Royce for Spain as well as one at home,' Lee told Will. 'Because look, the steering wheel is on the other side, the way it should be for here. If it was their British car it would be on the right-hand side.'

'Man, they must be *so* loaded!'

The tanned man shook hands with each member

of the Perfect Family before speaking briefly with the chauffeur and returning to his car. A few seconds later Mr and Mrs Perfect were holding onto their hats as the Rolls Royce pulled away, following behind the Ferrari.

'Well there's no doubt now,' Will said. 'They're definitely millionaires.'

But it didn't stop there. The Perfects weren't the only ones out and about in fancy cars. A bright yellow super car rumbled out of the hotel's underground car park. Everyone knew it was pulling out because its roof was down and music was booming from it. The bass thudded as if there was a rock concert going on outside the hotel-room door. Whoever was inside the car was not shy.

And Lee and Will immediately recognised the two figures filling the front seats. It was not even necessary to see their faces; the glint off their clothing made them immediately recognisable.

'The suits,' Will muttered.

'So it is.' Lee stretched forward over the railings.

'Careful,' Will warned. 'Don't fall over.'

'Do you think they have a whole case full of the same sorts of suits?' Lee mused.

'Looks like it.'

'Glad I'm not paying their dry cleaning bill.'

Rebecca's laughter floated out to them. Uncle Raymond was tickling her, something she loved and hated in equal doses, which was why she was laughing while trying to escape. At the same time, the yellow super car, which had been rumbling slowly along the road, shot off at speed, tyres screeching.

'There they go,' Will said, stating the obvious. 'Showing off all the way.'

'I wonder where they're going?' Lee mused.

'And what they're going to do when they get there.'

'Something they shouldn't be doing, I'll bet.

Something illegal.'

'They're definitely a dodgy pair.'

'Yeah, more dodgy than …' Will couldn't think of an ending for his sentence.

'… than two other really dodgy things,' Lee finished for him.

'Yeah,' Will said, finding some inspiration. 'More dodgy than two dodgem cars at a fairground.'

'And they've left at exactly the same time as The Perfects. Coincidence or …'

Will was ahead of him. '… Or are they heading for the same place?'

Lee shrugged. 'Could be.'

'But they're not the same sorts of people at all. The suits are kind of scary, whereas the Perfects are … too perfect.'

'Which is scary in its own way,' Will said. 'They think they're so much better than everyone else.' He stuck his foot into the narrow gap in the balcony's railings. It almost became stuck and he had to pull hard to get it back out again.

'We need to keep an eye on everything,' Lee said. 'I can't help thinking that something here isn't right.'

DAY THREE

Lee's whole family were letting their hair down. Even those with short hair. Lee's dad – often a little uptight when he arrived home from work – and his mum – often a little uptight before she went to work because she was fretting as she tried to get Rebecca and/or Lee out of the door to nursery/school on time – were chilling out. They were enjoying being able to laze by the pool, read their books in the sun and have their meals cooked for them. That was what summer holidays were all about, taking a break from the strains of everyday life.

At least it was for them. What Lee wanted to know was: what new fun and excitement did this day have in store for *him*?

The day soon had a chance to explain.

Spying on the shiny suits and the hotel manager had completely slipped Lee's mind until Will reminded him.

It had also slipped Will's mind until he'd seen one of the men who had been wearing a shiny suit two days beforehand. The excitement of the previous day – the dreadful car, the dull village and the squash on the way home – had clearly affected his ability to think. Maybe his mind was on holiday as well as his body.

This time the shiny suit with the Welsh accent was not at the hotel bar or outside the manager's office, instead he was standing in the shade outside the hotel's main entrance, speaking quietly into a mobile phone.

Immediately Will's suspicions were raised. What was so secret that the man couldn't speak inside the hotel? And why was he speaking so quietly with his head down and one hand over the outside of the phone as if trying to mute his voice?

'He could just be speaking to one of his girlfriends,' Lee suggested when Will arrived back at the pool and whispered to him. 'Gangsters don't care who they lie to or what they lie about, so he's probably telling his girlfriend how much he loves her before going off to tell another girl exactly the same thing.'

'Would you believe anything a man like that told you?'

'*I* wouldn't. But then I'm not his girlfriend.'

Will was relieved to hear this.

Normally Lee's mum would be telling him that it was rude to whisper, but she was either too chilled out to bother or fast asleep. It was difficult to tell which as she lay on her sunlounger and soaked up the rays.

'Why don't we see if he's still hanging around?' Lee suggested, easing himself upright.

Will shrugged. 'Why not.'

They made their way through the bar to the reception area without setting eyes on their target. Will stuck his head out of the front doorway in case the man was on the phone again, but there was no sign of him, so he set off for a wander around the outside of the building. Meanwhile, Lee hovered outside the hotel manager's office, hoping to hear something going on.

'Anything?' Will asked when he returned.

'No. You?'

'I didn't see anyone, but I took a wander down into the car park, and that flashy yellow sports car is down there. It's a Lamborghini.'

'How do you know that's what it is? I didn't think you were into cars.'

'It says on the back.'

'Aw.'

'Do you think maybe these guys are drug dealers?'

'I hope not. Drug dealers are the scum off the Earth.'

'My mum says they don't care what they do or to whom. They sell people drugs knowing they'll ruin their lives.'

'Your mum's right. But if that's what this is all about ...'

'It's heavy stuff, isn't it. I'm not sure we should get involved.'

'Just what I was thinking.'

'Although if everyone took that attitude, the dealers would always get away with being criminals.'

'There is that,' Lee said, not wanting to appear too cowardly. 'In which case maybe we should try to put a stop to what they're doing. We might save some lives if we do.'

'So maybe we should make a stand.'

'Yeah ...'

'Though it could be dangerous.'

'True.'

'So we could end up in deep trouble, getting hurt or kidnapped or whatever.'

'Well maybe it would be better if we ...'

'But we really ought to think of others, not just ourselves ...' Will said.

'Hang on a minute. I'm confused. Are you saying we should find out what's going on or we shouldn't?'

'I'm saying ... I don't know.'

'I thought as much.'

'But probably we should. It could be important.'

'You really are Mr Decisive, aren't you.'

'I don't know,' Will said before adding, 'Only joking.'

'Let's …' But Lee stopped in mid sentence and started walking quickly towards the bar area.

'Lee …' Will set off after him. He had only taken a few steps before he saw what Lee had already seen. The Welshman was walking in through the front door.

'It's alright, he's not after us,' Will said as he caught up with Lee, who had reached a pillar and was hiding behind it while at the same time trying to look casual and unconcerned.

'Phew, I thought maybe he was on to us.'

'Why would he be? We're just a couple of kids mucking about on holiday.'

Lee looked around. Will's point was a fair one. They weren't the only kids in the hotel. Plenty of others were inside, escaping the sun. The younger ones were charging about, climbing through the gaps in bar stools as if tackling an obstacle course. Older kids were playing the games machines. A couple of families were playing snakes and ladders and one was playing dominoes. Will was right, he and Lee weren't standing out from the crowd; they just felt they were.

Will was keeping an eye on the Welshman. He watched him approach the reception desk, take off his sunglasses and speak briefly with the receptionist, who handed him a key card. He then headed for the lift.

'Come on,' Will said. 'Let's follow him.'

After a moment's hesitation Lee left the safety of the pillar and the pair meandered over towards the lifts.

'I'm not getting in the same lift as him,' Lee said.

'Me neither.'

The lift arrived with a ding, the doors slid open with a clank and the Welshman stepped in, clearing his throat noisily as he did so.

'Where's he going to spit that out?' Lee asked.

'I don't know, but I'm never again stepping foot in any of the hotel lifts in my bare feet.'

In the time that it took the second lift to arrive, the polar ice caps melted, two continents joined together and man evacuated Earth because of the effects of global warming and went to live in another solar system. At least that was how long it seemed to take. But then it always takes things ages when you need them most.

Eventually the doors parted and they stepped inside.

'Which floor?' Lee asked.

'Ah. I don't know.'

'Well you've got a choice of one to ten.'

'We should have listened to see if we could work out which floor he stopped on.'

'We should have, but we didn't. So we'll need to try each one in turn.'

'He'll probably have disappeared into a room by the time we get there.'

'He will if you don't make a decision quickly.'

'Start at the top then.'

'Okay,' Lee said, pressing the button for the tenth floor. 'Although this doesn't make sense, does it. If he's gone to floor two it will have taken him hardly any time and we'll be miles behind him.'

'True.'

'You're supposed to be the genius, not me. But let's stick with it anyway.'

Lee whiled away the short journey by checking himself out in the mirror on the lift's back wall. No tan so far, but he was starting to get a bit of colour. Or was it just the light …?

The doors opened before he could decide. A big number '10' on the wall opposite announced that they were on the floor they intended to be on. Lee stuck his head around the corner of the metal door and looked left. Nothing. Then he looked right … and saw the Welshman wrestling with the door.

'He's there,' Lee told Will. 'And he's trying to break in.'

'Why would he do that? He collected a key from Reception. Let me see.' Will moved Lee to one side so he could look without having to step out of the lift. 'He's not breaking in,' Will reported. 'He just can't get the key to work.'

'Aw.'

'He must be staying here. But if he is, why have we never seen him down at the pool? Why does he spend the whole time in a suit?'

'Maybe …' Lee was cut short by Will clattering into him as the door decided to close itself. 'Woah!' And then the lift was descending. Lee prodded the button for the ninth floor and they came to a halt. He intended to return them to the tenth floor again, but when the doors opened they were confronted by a pretty young cleaner accompanied by a trolley laden with cloths, sprays, soaps and toilet rolls.

'Allo' she said.

'Hi,' the two boys replied at the same time. And that was it, conversation over. They knew no more Spanish and if the cleaner knew any English she was avoiding using it. They all stood in silence until Lee suddenly jumped out into the corridor. 'Come on,' he prompted Will, who leapt after him, leaving the cleaner behind.

Lee and Will headed for the stairwell and bounded up the stairs, back to the top floor.

'Too late,' Lee said, having stuck his head around the

corner. 'He's gone.'

'But at least we know which room he's in.'

Lee nodded. 'I'm not sure what that tells us.'

'It tells us that whatever he's doing, he's doing it in that room.'

As lunchtime approached it was hot enough for bread to toast itself and for eggs to cook themselves, which was handy if you fancied a fry up. It was certainly too hot to lie about, so Uncle Raymond and Lee's dad decided to swim to the bar in the middle of the pool. Lee and Will followed.

Uncle Raymond was a good swimmer. He dived in to the glinting, rippling water and moved sleekly through it like a porpoise, surfacing just short of the bar.

Lee's dad was a decidedly poorer swimmer but felt the need to follow his brother-in-law's lead. He half-dived, half-jumped, half-staggered into the pool, belly flopping as he did so, and came up coughing and spluttering and spitting out the water that had shot up his nostrils.

Lee tried not to laugh, but failed.

'I'll bet that hurt,' Will said to Lee's dad.

'No, no, not really,' Lee's dad said, short of breath and holding his reddening stomach but unwilling to admit he'd made a fool of himself. 'I was only doing it for effect. Sounded worse than it felt.' He spat out some more water.

Uncle Raymond was sitting waiting for the three of them on a submerged seat. 'Right, what are we all having?' he asked.

The barman said hi. 'My name is Amador,' he announced.

Uncle Raymond leaned over the bar, hand outstretched. 'Pleased to meet you,' he told the dark-haired young Spaniard. 'We must be related. I'm a window.'

Lee and Will burst out laughing. It took Amador a few seconds to get the joke, but he laughed too once he'd got it. (He had to laugh; these were paying customers.)

They ordered drinks. Another two men were occupying the only other seats at the bar. Each was nursing a golden beer in a plastic glass.

'How do they get the drinks over here?' Lee wondered aloud. 'Does someone have to swim over with them?'

'I guess so,' his dad said.

'We carry the crates above our heads,' Amador added, having heard Lee's question and handing him and Will the colas they'd asked for.

Lee's dad said to the barman, 'I take it Amador's only your name when you're closed. Presumably when you're open, you're Amajar.'

This joke (like so many of Lee's dad's) was so bad that Lee, Will and Uncle Raymond considered drowning themselves on the spot to escape it. 'Dad, that's dreadful,' Lee said. 'And,' Uncle Raymond added, 'most of the dinosaurs heard that one before they became extinct.'

'Maybe hearing it was what *caused* them to become extinct,' Will suggested. 'Maybe it wasn't Earth colliding with a comet after all.'

Amador had no idea what they were on about. 'Amajar?' he queried. 'What is Amajar?'

As was often the case (such as when tasting the wine the day before), Lee's dad didn't know when to stop. 'When a door's open it's ajar,' he tried to explain. But Amador was still confused. 'I no understand. How can wooden door become glass jar?'

'Well …' Lee's dad was all for trying another explanation but Uncle Raymond intervened, saying, 'Would you look at that?'

Lee's dad (along with Lee and Will) turned around. 'What?' they all said together.

'Nothing. But that's still more interesting than your attempts at an explanation.'

Fortunately Lee's dad could laugh at himself, which, given that others spent a lot of time laughing at him, was just as well, otherwise he could have spent much of his life feeling left out.

'So have you found any other kids to get up to no good with?' Uncle Raymond asked Lee and Will.

'Not really,' Will said.

'That's a shame. That's what I always liked about the summer holidays – getting up to all sorts of things that we weren't supposed to get up to.'

'What sorts of things?' Lee asked.

'Oh, well, like … let me see now … ehm …'

'That doesn't sound too rebellious,' Lee's dad pointed out.

'We used to ride on the tops of haystacks once they'd been loaded onto tractors,' Uncle Raymond said. 'God only knows what would have happened if we'd fallen off.'

'Didn't your parents stop you?' Will said.

'My Dad was too busy getting on with running the farm, and so was my mum come to think of it. That and looking after your mum, who was obviously much more trouble than me.'

'Some things never change,' Lee's dad mumbled.

'Dad, have you seen that the Perfect Family are here with us?'

'Yes, I heard you splashed them earlier on. Oh how my heart bled for the poor souls.'

Will grinned. He'd been trying to think up other ways

of annoying them, but so far had drawn a blank. It would only be a matter of time, however, if he concentrated hard enough.

Meanwhile, Lee explained to his uncle how the Perfect Family had behaved on the flight over.

'I say, Old Bean. Are they a bunch of snooty toffs, or what?'

Lee and Will nodded, smiling. Then, as if on cue, Perfect Father stepped stiffly out of the hotel and marched over to rejoin his Perfect Family at the poolside, rearranging his cap as he walked.

'Well, anyone who thinks they're better than anyone else usually gets their comeuppance in the end. So let's hope this lot are no different and their comeuppance comes sooner rather than later.'

It would if Lee and Will had anything to do with it.

The music around the pool changed suddenly. Ever since they'd arrived the discreet speakers had been pumping out pop and rock songs. That suited Lee well, it was just the sort of music he loved. So why had they changed it to classical music?

'What's going on?' he asked, sitting up on the sunlounger he'd returned to.

Will had been engrossed in a book, but put it to one side. 'I've no idea.'

'Let's ask Amador,' Lee suggested. Will shrugged, rolled off the sunlounger and stood up. Lee joined him and, after checking there was no one in the spot they were aiming for, they dived into the pool. Even though the water was actually quite warm, it felt cold when you had been frying in the sun. If you went into the pool slowly it was like torture. The only thing to do was get your whole body in as quickly as possible, which was why diving was best.

It was Amador who controlled the music that was played around the pool. Lee knew this because he had seen the barman changing CDs when they had been at the pool bar before. Only he could have changed the music. The question was: why had he done so?

'Hi Amador,' Lee called as he and Will pulled themselves out of the water and onto a pair of vacant stools.

'You two are like dolphins swimming through the water,' the barman declared.

'Thanks,' Will told him.

'You reckon?' Lee said, enjoying the compliment.

Amador grinned. 'Yes. You both have very long noses and make strange sounds. Ha ha! Now, what can I get you?'

'Nothing, thanks. We were just wondering what's going on with the music.'

Amador's smile disappeared. 'Someone complained.'

'Complained about what? The music you were playing was great. We loved it.'

'Yes, I agree, it was good music. But this man ...' Amador moved his head and eyes just enough to make clear the corner of the pool he meant, '... he complained that it was too noisy and that there was no classical music. He didn't say to me, he said to the hotel manager.'

'Did the manager give you the CD?'

'No, the man did. He had it with him.'

Will chipped in. 'If it was someone over there ...' He nodded to where Amador had indicated, '... there's only one man it could be.'

'Perfect Father.'

'Exactly. Who else would complain about this sort of thing?'

Who else indeed. Perfect Father was really starting to get on Lee's nerves.

'You're not going to play his music all of the time, though, are you?' Will asked Amador.

'No, no. Only a little bit when he is here. No other time.'

'Well I suppose that's something. If we get to hear our kind of music, he should get to hear his. He's paid for his holiday like everyone else.'

Lee thought Will was going soft. 'Yeah, except he's got a penthouse suite and a maid and all the rest.'

'It's still fair that he gets to hear a bit of what he likes. We wouldn't like it if we had to listen to classical music all day, so if he doesn't want to listen to rock all the time then that's fine by me. As long as it's not on for long.'

'One CD only,' Amador told them.

'Hmm,' Lee said, not convinced. 'He can certainly afford to buy some more.'

'He can buy, but it is me who plays them.'

'Good.'

'So what do you want to drink?'

'Eh, nothing. We just came to see what was happening with the music.'

'Ah. There I was thinking you had come specially to see me.'

'Well, yeah. Kind of.'

'Well you can't sit at my bar and just talk. Other people might want to come. You need to have a drink.'

'Aw. I'd need to check with my dad …'

'Here,' Amador said. He reached into the fridge and brought out two drinks. 'But don't tell anyone. Especially not the hotel manager.' He winked at them as he placed two plastic cups on the bar.

'Thanks, Amador,' Will said.

'Yeah, cheers,' Lee added.

'And cheers to you,' Amador replied. 'Cheers Big Ears.'

Lee and Will laughed. Lee sprayed some of his drink out of his nose and onto the bar. Will choked on his.

They sat there for ten minutes, until other customers arrived, then they swam back to the side of the pool and climbed out. Lee was just about to sit down on his sunlounger when a voice called, 'You want to play water polo?' Lee turned round to see a blond kid holding a ball in one hand.

'Why don't you?' Uncle Raymond encouraged.

Why not, Lee thought, even though it had been exhausting the last time. He and Will jumped back into the water and were soon doing their best to get the ball between the markers on the edge of the pool.

The blond kid turned out to be Dutch, as his older sister explained once most of the others had drifted away, back to their families. She spoke English and Lee felt a little embarrassed because he didn't know a single word of Dutch, not even 'please' or 'thank you'.

The girl and her brother were from Amsterdam and lived on a houseboat on one of the main canals. Lee loved the idea of living on a big boat, but Will wasn't so convinced. 'I went on a ferry once and felt sick.'

'Houseboats don't move!' the girl exclaimed.

'Oh right.'

Three other kids were still with them. They were from Ireland and, with their thick accents, Lee and Will at first found it easier to make out what the Dutch girl and boy were saying, but their ears soon tuned in.

'What are your names?' the Dutch girl asked the Irish kids.

The eldest, a girl, introduced them all. 'This is Paula,' she said, pointing to an impish girl with so many freckles on her cheeks that if she could join them all up she'd have a fabulous instant tan. 'And this is

Padraig.' She nodded at a skinny boy who'd been one of the most energetic swimmers in the pool during their water-polo game.

'What sort of a name is Porridge?' Lee asked. 'Scottish?' Memories of the wallpaper-paste-like breakfast mush his parents had forced him to try at a hotel during their Scottish tour came flooding back. They weren't happy memories.

'Not Porridge, you dummy,' the girl said. 'Padraig.' She spelt it out for him.

'Aw.'

'You just pronounce it as if it's PAW-RICK.'

'Aw.'

'Couldn't you just spell it that way, then?' Will asked.

'It's Gaelic,' the girl explained.

'But I thought you were Irish,' the Dutch girl said, confused. 'You are Gaelic?'

'No, no. We're Irish. But Padraig's name is Gaelic. Lots of Irish names are.'

'Oh, I understand.'

Paula pointed to her elder sister, who was wearing a bright pink bikini and matching beads at the end of the braids in her light brown hair. 'And she's Carmel.'

'Like they put in toffee?' Will asked.

'Not quite the same spelling,' Carmel pointed out, 'but close, I suppose.'

The Dutch girl told them all her name was Anna, and her brother was Ben.

'How come your English is so good?' Paula asked Anna.

'We learn it in school from when we are very young. Ben has learned some English, too, but he is not as old.'

Ben clearly felt the need to show off what he had learned. 'I am nine,' Ben said very precisely. 'How old are you being?'

'I'm seven,' Paula announced. Anna said she was eleven, the same age as Carmel. It seemed to Lee that both girls were older than that, but sometimes that was the way with girls; they could be old before their years.

A woman called out something unintelligible. 'That is our mother,' Anna said. 'We must go now. We are going touristing.'

They all knew what she meant and didn't correct her.

'We see you here tomorrow, yes?'

Everyone said they would.

The Irish kids had been at the hotel two days longer than Lee and Will.

'Have you been exploring, Lads?' asked Padraig.

'A bit,' Lee lied. 'Not very much, though,' he added, which was getting closer to the truth.

'We've taken the hotel owner's dog for a walk,' Paula stated.

'You mean, it took you for a walk,' her sister pointed out.

'It did not. I told it where to go.'

'Yes, I'm sure you did, but it ignored you and went its usual route instead.'

'Anyway, it's a lovely dog, so it is,' Paula said.

'It's a manky rat,' Padraig told them all. 'I wouldn't be surprised if it has fleas all over it.' Then, turning to Paula, he said, 'And I've seen you scratchin' a bit as well.'

'No I haven't.'

'Sure you have, hasn't she, Carmel.'

'That's just the sunburn because she didn't put her sun cream on. Sure, Da's got it too, all over his back.'

'Come on, Lads,' Padraig said. 'We'll show you where you can get lemons and limes off the trees.'

Lee and Will didn't even know what a lime actually

looked like, so they were keen to see one.

They climbed out of the pool, dried off and told Lee's mum they were going off with the Irish kids. 'Don't go too far,' she warned, as all mums do, because that's what it tells them to do in their *How to Bring Up Children* book, available at all good bookshops or for free by sending away five tokens off the side of a cereal box. His dad and Uncle Raymond were inside playing pool. Lee's dad had yet to win a game, Lee's mum reported. 'But he's determined to, so they'll probably be playing in there for the rest of the day.'

The Irish kids were full of energy. They showed Lee and Will where to climb over a fence as a short cut to the next hotel, then led them round the side to where a few less modern apartments were located alongside the main hotel building. Outside each doorway was a tree, and on each one hung stacks of round, vibrant green limes the size of plums.

'Can you eat them?' Lee asked.

'Not on their own,' Carmel told him. 'They're sour. You put them in things when you're cooking. Or put them in drinks to give them extra taste.'

'Can we take one?'

'If you want. There are some lying on the ground where they've fallen off.'

Lee and Will lunged forward into the grass, which needed a cut.

'But, Lads, watch out for the big snakes!' Padraig called.

Lee and Will stopped in their tracks. 'Snakes?' they asked together.

'Yeah. In the grass.'

Lee and Will looked at each other, unsure whether to stay where they were, go forward or go back.

'He's only kidding,' Carmel called. Lee and Will ran on to the nearest tree. Carmel continued: 'The snakes aren't all *that* big. And they're only a little bit poisonous.'

There were several limes on the ground, their waxy green peels reflecting the sun. Lee picked one up after checking the nearby grass to make sure a snake wasn't going to dart out from under a clump and bite his hand. There was something special about holding fruit that was fresh from a tree instead of from a supermarket shelf. Picking it off the ground gave Lee a caveman feeling; the sense that he could, if he needed to, fend for himself, living off the trees and bushes and wildlife that nature had provided as humankind's means of survival.

Then again, he could carry on taking food from the freezer and nuking it in the microwave, which was a whole lot easier and less likely to result in you starving to death.

Lee gathered up three prime examples of limes to take back and show his family. Then he and Will rejoined the others.

'Come on, let's go to the beach,' Padraig encouraged. 'Have you been down? There are loads of nudie women there.'

'Padraig!' his big sister scolded, then walked on ahead with Paula.

'There are though, Lads,' Padraig whispered behind his sisters' backs. 'Honest. Hundreds of them. All nudie. My da couldn't keep his eyes off them.'

Lee and Will weren't sure they wanted to see what Padraig had described, but didn't want to admit it to Padraig, who was, after all, younger than them.

'Have you seen the Perfect Family?' Lee asked Padraig.

'The what?'

'The Perfect Family. They've been round the pool. The guy wears a stupid flat cap …'

'Oh them! What a bunch of eejits they are. Sure, I asked the kids if they wanted to play water polo with the rest of us, but they just looked at me as if I'd come down from another planet.'

'You probably weren't speaking poshly enough for them,' Will told him.

'There's nothing wrong with the way I speak.'

'I just mean that they only understand people who speak as if they're members of the Royal Family.'

'We haven't got a royal family back home,' Padraig said.

'My dad reckons we shouldn't have one either,' Lee said. 'He's always ranting on about it. "Why should some old biddy, who just happens to be the daughter of the last king, be in charge of the whole country?" he says.'

'She's not really in charge, though, is she,' Will said.

'Well she gets all the castles and all the money, so she's got herself a great deal if she's not actually having to run everything.'

Hearing that the conversation had moved on, Carmel and Paula rejoined them.

'How come you haven't got royalty in Ireland?' Will asked.

'Because,' Carmel said, 'the last royal family to rule over Ireland was the English one. They invaded us and told everyone what they could and couldn't do. Strangely enough, that wasn't very popular, so ever since the English left we've had a president instead. Someone the people of Ireland have chosen to represent them.'

'Maybe your da should move to Ireland,' Padraig suggested. 'Maybe he'd be happier there, with it not having any poncy royals.'

Quite possibly, Lee thought.

'Anyway, what were you saying about that family?'

Carmel asked.

'Just that they're a bunch of stuck-up toffs.'

'Too right.'

'What can we do to upset them?' Lee asked, eager to stir things up.

'Tell them the Queen's died?' Paula suggested.

'Put arsenic in their water?' Padraig said.

'A bit extreme,' Will told him, and Carmel agreed.

A thought came to Lee. 'Why don't we do something with their room? We could follow them when they go up and see where they're staying.'

'And then put cockroaches in their fridge,' Will proposed. 'If they can survive a nuclear bomb, then they'll be able to survive in a fridge. They might even like it; they can cool down out of the heat.'

Carmel looked at her waterproof watch. 'We should go down to the beach quickly, and then get back before they go up.'

'Oh yah,' Lee said in his poshest voice. 'They'll probably go up quite early, so they can change into their robes and tiaras and have cocktails before dinner, as one does.'

It was agreed, and after a quick walk along the beach, mostly spent with Padraig pointing out nudie women that were of little interest to Lee or Will, all five of them returned to the pool just as Lee's parents, sister and uncle were all packing up.

'Did you have a good time?' Lee's dad asked.

'Oh yes, we saw some very interesting sights,' Lee said, nudging Will.

'That's right, Will said. 'Some amazing, eh, dunes.'

'Oh, well that's good,' his mum said. 'And that's great that you've made some friends, too.'

It was. The Irish kids had briefly rejoined their own family, who were also packing up their things now that the sun was melting into the horizon.

'Mum, we're just going to stay out a bit longer and play with them,' Lee said, indicating Carmel, Padraig and little Paula.

Lee's mum was collecting together the various books, creams, sandals and sunglasses that were spread out around the three sunloungers the adults had been using. 'Okay, but don't be too long.'

'We won't be,' Lee told her, and he and Will scampered round the pool to join the others, where they were introduced to the Irish kids' mum and dad.

'How's it going, Lads?' their dad asked.

'Yeah, great,' Will answered for them both.

'Ah, that's grand. I hear Padraig's been showing you all the nudie women down on the beach, is that right?'

Lee and Will thought maybe Padraig's dad was fishing for information with which to get Padraig into trouble, so they stalled while they blushed. 'Eh, well …'

'Sure, some of them are a grand sight, right enough. You can't get enough of nudie women, now, can you. Nudie women and Guinness. It's what the world was made for.'

'Come on now, Sean,' the kids' mother said to their dad. 'You're embarrassing those two. Don't be messing with them.'

Carmel took this as a prompt to hasten Lee and Will away. 'Da's just having a laugh with you,' she said.

'See you around, Lads!' the Irish kids' dad called loudly as he went off. Lee and Will waved.

The Perfect Family was by now also tidying up to go. Lee pointed out to the others that the woman's hair never moved, even when she bent over. 'Do you think it's real?' he asked as they sat under a palm tree, watching.

'It's probably made of cardboard,' Padraig said.

'She'd better watch out it doesn't catch fire in the heat,' Will commented, and they all sniggered at the image of her running about after her hair had suddenly caught fire.

'She'd have to dive into the pool to put it out,' Paula said, laughing.

Finally the Perfect Family made their move, which was the cue Lee, Will and the three Irish kids had been waiting for to make theirs, too.

'What do you think their room will be like?' Padraig asked.

Lee had a clear idea of what to expect. 'For a start, it won't be one room. They'll have several – a whole suite.'

'That's right,' Will said. 'The Presidential Suite.'

'Do they have one here?' Carmel asked.

'Don't all hotels have one? It'll either be that or a penthouse up at the top, with a big roof garden you can walk around.'

'I'll bet the bathrooms all have gold taps,' Paula said. 'And special ones with bubble bath coming out of them.'

'And four-poster beds with silk sheets.'

'And air conditioning so you don't sweat all night when you're trying to get to sleep.'

'And TVs everywhere.'

'Yeah, ones that have programmes that aren't all in Spanish.'

'And loads of sweet machines that you don't even need money for.'

'And a huge games room with every toy imaginable in it.'

The Perfect Family had, of course, taken the lift. One of their staff must have seen them coming and arranged for the lift to be waiting for them as they entered the reception area, complete with its shiny marbly floor.

Lee, Will and the Irish kids climbed the stairs in a hurry, their imaginations running riot. As they reached each floor they checked if the lift had stopped.

Eventually they heard a ding above them. 'At last!' Lee panted. He and Will were slightly ahead of the others.

'It had to be this one,' Will panted back. 'This is the tenth and top floor!'

'The same one as before,' Lee muttered as he tried to catch his breath. 'The Perfects and the shiny suits on the same floor.'

The Irish kids caught up, but then they all had to pile back round the corner at the half-landing as the Perfect Family left the lift and pranced towards them along the corridor, passing the top of the stairs.

The five kids crept forward again, eager to see which room the Perfect Family would enter and whether a butler would welcome them.

The Perfects stopped and Mr Perfect reached for a door knob. At that very moment the door opened and a woman stepped out. A brief conversation ensued, one which Lee, Will and the others could not make out, after which the woman walked towards the lifts.

'Quick, back again!' Lee warned.

Once they were safely round the corner of the stairs Will said, 'They must let their staff off in the evening once the meals are made and the dinner clothes have all been ironed.'

'Or maybe that maid's just finished her stint and the nightshift people are already inside.'

They heard another ding, followed by the opening and closing of the lift doors.

'There must be servants' quarters somewhere,' Lee said. 'Probably on a different floor.'

'But what could that maid have been doing all day?'

Carmel asked. 'Babysitting Perfect Daughter's dolls?'

Paula liked this idea. 'She might have been, because the dolls weren't at the pool, so they'd get lonely up here in a country they don't know.'

Padraig raised his eyebrows, which Lee and Will took to mean *You know how it is with little sisters*, which Lee certainly did because he had one and she was into dolls as well, though he'd hoped she'd be past that stage well before Paula's age. Now he had his doubts. It seemed girls could be fascinated by dollies for years, probably right up until when they replaced them with real babies.

'What are we going to do?' Carmel asked.

'Walk along the corridor,' Lee stated. 'It's a free country and there aren't any No Entry signs. What's to stop us?'

'Lads, maybe they'll have armed guards,' Padraig suggested enthusiastically, clearly hoping he was correct.

'I doubt it,' his big sister said. 'If they didn't have them down at the pool, why would they have them up here?'

'Because this is where they keep all their gold and their jewels for wearing at night, and they might be worried that people will break in and nick it all.'

'People like us, you mean?' Carmel said.

'Yes,' Padraig told her.

'We're not going to steal anything from them,' Lee said. 'Just have a laugh.'

'But *they* don't know that.'

'Come on,' Will said. 'Let's not hang about, let's get going.'

They scrabbled back up the stairs and walked along the corridor.

'They look just like ours,' Paula said as they passed by each door with its plastic number stuck to it.

'Ah, but that's so you won't realise they're special

rooms and get jealous,' Padraig said.

'But don't all rich people like to show off what they've got?'

'Not all of them,' Lee told her. 'Some like to keep it a secret so others won't want some of what they've got.'

They were whispering by now because they were nearing the door the Perfect Family had entered. Lee pointed at it. Number 1066.

The meaning of this was immediately clear to Will. 'Look, they must be royalty! 1066 was the year of the Battle of Hastings, when William the Conquerer, who was the Duke of Normandy, a place in France, took over England by beating King Harold the second – the one who got his eye poked out by an arrow.' (Will was good at history.) 'He also wrote the Doomsday Book, but I hear the plot is rubbish.'

'There's not much we can do while they're in there,' Carmel said.

'No,' Lee agreed. 'Let's go. We'll come back tomorrow.'

So they left the ordinary-looking door behind and headed back to their own rooms to rejoin their parents.

Lee's mum insisted on wearing socks and shoes in the apartment because of the cockroach incident. She now also insisted that Lee and Will write some postcards.

'If you don't write them now, before we go out for dinner,' she said, 'you'll be back home before they are.' She held out a brown paper bag. 'Here you go. I've bought a stack for you. All you need to do is write them.'

All they needed to do was write them. Writing them

was the difficult bit!

'Who have I got to send them to?' Lee asked.

'Your granny and grandpa, and your gran. Plus you'd better send one to Aunt Liz.'

'That's loads!'

'Lee, that's precisely three postcards. I'm sure you can manage that given all that they do for you. And they always take time out from their holiday to write you one.'

She had a point there.

So Lee sat out on the balcony and tried to think what to write. But after five minutes all he could come up with was:

Dear Granny and Grandpa,

Weather good, wish you were here!

Love from Lee

Neither very exciting nor original, he had to admit, but he couldn't think of anything else, so he wrote the words in large letters so they'd fill up all the space on the postcard, and then did another one the same for his gran. If his mum read the card and asked him about it, he'd say he had to write big because his granny and grandpa were old and couldn't read small writing – he'd only been trying to ensure they didn't get eye strain trying to read what he'd written.

Two down, one to go. What could he write on the one to Aunt Liz, Uncle Raymond's partner? (She wasn't strictly an aunt, but that was what they called her any-way.) After another couple of minutes thinking, still the only thing filling his head was the bright sun. Then he had a brainwave.

Dear Aunt Liz,

Weather here, wish you were good!

Love from Lee

That would do nicely. Same words, different order. What a genius! It was probably the sort of silly card that Uncle Raymond would send her anyway, and she could take a joke (which, given that she lived with his uncle, was really just as well).

'Finished!' he said to his mum as he walked back inside.

'That was quick,' she said.

'My ideas were flowing today,' Lee explained like a budding author. He'd already put the stamps on and addressed the cards, so he handed them to his mum picture-side up so she wouldn't see what he'd written.

Will was writing a card to his mum. 'Can I see what you've written?' Lee said. Will handed it to him.

Dear Mum and Dad,

We are here now and it's nice, but it's only a few days til we head back again, which isn't nice.

The weather has been nice, and the pool is nice too, and so is the food.

We've met some nice friends and are having a nice time with them.

Love Will

Will's writing was tiny so that he could fit all the words into the space available.

'That's eh, nice,' Lee said.

'Maybe I've used *nice* too much,' Will said. 'I was lacking inspiration.'

'Hmm. I see what you mean. Maybe you've overused it just a bit.'

Fortunately Will had written his postcard in pencil, so he was able to rub out some of the 'nice' words and replace them with nicer ones.

DAY FOUR

'Do you realise we're halfway through our holiday already?!' Lee asked incredulously, hiding the fingers he'd been counting on. 'Halfway! We've had four nights here and it's a seven night holiday. What they don't tell you in the brochure is that seven nights means only six days.'

Rebecca was totally confused and Will was struggling to follow. 'How do you work that out?' he said.

'The first night was the one at the end of the day we travelled here,' Lee said. 'And after the seventh night we've got to go home. So we lose a day. Well, sort of.'

'You've been thinking too much,' Uncle Raymond said. 'You want to watch out for that. It'll give you a big forehead.'

'Yeah, but it's depressing. I feel as if I've only just arrived, and now we'll soon have to go back again.'

'Well, not just yet,' his dad said brightly. 'And anyway, you've still got three full days to go, so let's make the most of them.'

'What are we doing today then?' Will asked.

'We're going to the water park.'

'Alright!' Lee and Will cried together. So did Rebecca before asking, 'Dad, what's a water park?'

'It's like a park, only with lots of water.'

'Hooray!' Only, the more she thought about this the less sense it made. 'But how will the swings swing? And won't the flowers drown?'

Lee's mum put her right and a smile spread across Rebecca's face.

An even bigger smile had already spread across Lee's face. 'Oh yes, Dad! Thanks. This is what I've really really wanted to do all holiday.' Will followed on behind as Lee dashed off to get his swimming shorts.

They were taken to the water park in a minibus that was old and battered and had seats that stuck to your legs like cling film. But that was still a huge improvement on the old wreck of a rental car, which Lee had been worried they might have to travel in again.

It was still early in the day when they arrived at the water park. This was just as Lee's dad had planned. He wanted to avoid the queues that would undoubtedly build as the day wore on.

As they entered through the main gates, Lee and Will marvelled at the size of some of the slides. 'Look at that one!' Lee said.

'It's humungous!' Will agreed.

'Massive!'

'Ginormous!'

'And scary,' Lee said. 'I'm not going up that. Not for all the jewels in room 1066.'

'Come on, don't be such a big woose,' Uncle Raymond chided. 'You can do that. Look!'

The slide looked to Lee and Will as if it would tower over Mount Everest if placed next to it. A kid about their age was at the top, looking over tentatively to see what was below. Lee's dad was encouraging them to move on and get in a queue, but Lee and Will wanted to see what happened to the kid at the top, because they knew that if he did it, they would be obliged to do it too, and that was a prospect they were relishing about as much as cabbage ice cream with liquidised snail sauce, which Uncle Raymond had insisted, at dinner the previous evening, was a delicacy in this part of Spain.

Some mates of the boy at the top were helpfully giving him a countdown. 'Five, four, three, two, one …'

Nothing. The kid moved forward but didn't let go of the handles at the side, so he stayed exactly where he was.

A queue was building up below him and the pressure was on. 'Come on!' someone shouted impatiently. Lee wondered if that person would be quite so impatient at the front of the queue.

There were two lanes and now a man climbed into the lane next to the kid, and, after another countdown, he let go and down he went, going 'Aghhhhhhhh …' most of the way down, then 'Oooooh …' when he reached the bottom. He was still going 'Oooooh …' when he stood up. Such had been the force of the water and slide beneath him that half of his shorts appeared to have disappeared up his backside. He tried to retrieve them, then checked that nothing at the front – nothing that might be rather essential to his life – had disappeared, too.

'Look at that!' Rebecca hollered, pointing to another slide. Of course, at that moment the kid their age let go and hurtled down the enormously steep slide, and Lee and Will missed it all.

Still, the slide Rebecca was pointing at looked well worth a go. It had a fully enclosed flume so you were in a tunnel to start with, then at the bottom, when you came out of the tunnel, you went round and round in a bit shaped like a pudding bowl, only this one had a hole in the bottom that you eventually fell through, into a pool of water.

'Are you going to have a go?' Lee asked his mum.

'Hmm. We'll see. Later, maybe.'

Lee's dad and his Uncle Raymond were definitely up

for having a go. 'Come on,' they nagged, desperate to get to the first slide. The one they had in mind wasn't anywhere near as steep as the one where the man's shorts had disappeared up his backside, but the start of it wasn't much lower. It had four lanes that took you fleeing down to the bottom. Watching those already coming down the slide, it was clear that you took off into the air where the slope suddenly got steeper.

'That looks so cool,' Uncle Raymond said. 'Come on, Fiona! Go for it! Show the kids what you're made of!'

It appeared that Lee's mum was made of jelly, because she was shaking at the thought of flying down the ride. Given the temperature, she certainly couldn't claim it was the cold. 'I think I'll start on something gentler,' she said. 'Eh, just so Rebecca's not left out with the things she goes on.'

'But Mum,' the fearless Rebecca said, 'I want to go on that one with Dad.'

'Oh look, what a shame.' Lee's mum pointed at a sign. 'It says that you have to be that height to go on.' *That height* was a good bit above Rebecca's current height. It was even close to Lee's.

'But Mum …'

'Sorry, those are the rules, Darling.' She shrugged. 'Nothing I can do.'

So off went Lee, his dad, Will and Uncle Raymond. And they had a brilliant time. No sooner had they finished terrifying themselves on one slide than they were running to the next.

'This is so good!' Will told Lee's dad. 'It's one of the best days I've ever had.'

Once they'd been on everything that wasn't too babyish for them, they met back up with Lee's mum and Rebecca who were playing on a small slide at the edge of the main pool.

'So, you've done everything else. Are you ready for

the challenge of The Big One now?' Uncle Raymond asked. 'The one we saw when we came in?'

Lee was swithering. Could he do it? He'd managed everything else. It was just a case of letting go and enjoying the ride.

'Shall we?' Will asked.

'Go on!' Uncle Raymond cried. 'You can do it!'

'Will you come too?' Lee asked his dad, who in turn looked at his mum, who in turn looked at Uncle Raymond.

'I suppose I'd better take a turn of looking after Rebecca,' Lee's dad said selflessly.

'No, no, it's okay, you go,' Lee's mum told her husband. 'I honestly don't mind.'

'Fiona, I know you're just saying that. I know you really want to go, even if it's just to watch and make sure Lee and Will and Raymond are all okay. I really ought to stay with Rebecca. She'll be wondering who I am by now.'

'I hardly think so …'

'Okay, you cowards,' Uncle Raymond conceded. 'I'll go with them. One of us had better. Right, come on you two, let's do it.'

From the bottom of the steps it looked a long way up. From the top, it looked a hundred times further back down.

'Great views, eh?' Uncle Raymond asked.

'Oh, yes, marvellous,' Lee replied. 'I could stay up here all day.'

'So could I,' Will said. 'It would sure beat having to go down the slide.'

'Ah, come on, it'll be fun.'

'Fun?' Lee said. 'It's not fun, it's scaring yourself half to death!'

The queue was shortening. As each person went over the top and into oblivion, Lee and Will's turns drew closer. To make matters worse, a young girl was sitting in a chair on the very top of the slide, looking down at those waiting to go and then making sure they didn't fall to their deaths as they went. Lee didn't find this the slightest bit reassuring. 'What's she meant to do if you do fall off?' Lee said to Will. 'Fly down like Superman and catch you in her arms before you smash your skull on the ground?'

But it wasn't just the fact that she wouldn't be able to help if things went wrong that was bothering Lee. She was a girl. Worse still, she was a girl who didn't look remotely bothered about sitting high up in a chair with the wind blowing in her hair, despite being on the very top of a ride so tall that if the moon were out Lee was sure he would have been able to reach out and touch it. And if that girl was perfectly comfortable there, how could Lee or Will back out when they got to the front of the queue? Because, if they did, it would mean they would have chickened out of something a girl wasn't scared of, and that just couldn't be allowed.

Two more bodies disappeared into the unknown. Lee and Will had joined separate queues, one for each lane. Now only one person stood in front of each of them. Lee leaned forward to view the slope of the slide, but it was too steep for him to be able to see its surface from where he stood.

Then the boys in front of them went down, meaning it was now Lee and Will's turn.

They edged forward, holding tightly to the rail.

'You been on this ride before?' the girl in the chair asked.

Lee and Will shook their heads.

'Okay, well keep your arms in and cross your legs.'

'Is that so you don't pee yourself?' Will asked Lee, who shrugged.

'Okay, move forward now and get ready to go,' the

girl called.

'Come on, Lee! Come on, Will!' Uncle Raymond hollered behind them.

Lee looked over the lip of the slide again, but this wasn't like one of those in the swing park where you could see all the way to the bottom. Even right at the edge you couldn't see where you were going. It was as if someone had come along and cut off the whole of the bit that was meant to support you on the way down. It was even worse when you sat; then you couldn't even see the bottom, just the rest of the park laid out before you and then the sea and then Africa miles away across the Mediterranean. No, surely he couldn't see Africa ….

Uncle Raymond was urging them on, as were most of those waiting for their own turn. 'Big countdown now. Ready? Five … four …' Lee crossed his fingers and his toes as well as his arms and his legs. ' … three, two …' He looked over at Will, but Will couldn't see him because he had his eyes closed. '… one …'

'Aaaaaaaaaaaaaaaaaaaaaaaaaaaaaagggggggggggggggggg hhhhhhhhhhhhhhhhhhhhhhhhhhhhhhhhhhhhhhhhhhhh-hhhhhhhhhhhh …'

'Lee?'

'Aaaaaaaaaaagggggggghhhhhhhhhhhhhhhhhhhhhhhh …'

'Lee?'

'Aaaaaaaaaaagggggggghhhhhhhhhhhhhhhhhhhhhhhh …'

'Lee, you can open your eyes now. We've got you lunch. It's hot dogs.'

Hot dogs! Lee cautiously opened one eye. It was true! There before him was a hot dog, the first he'd had since school had finished for the summer. Seeing it, he immediately opened his second eye.

'Oh, man,' he said, letting out a huge sigh of relief.

Will was next to him. 'Did we really do it?' Lee asked. Will nodded. He had temporarily lost the tan he'd been getting.

'You're a couple of very brave kids,' Uncle Raymond beamed. 'And I'm proud of you.'

'Thanks,' Lee said.

'You did it too, didn't you?' Lee asked his uncle.

'Of course. I came down right behind you. It was terrifying. I thought it was going to rip my …'

'How's your hot dog?' Lee's mum interrupted.

Lee looked at it. He'd had one bite. 'You know, I think I've left my stomach somewhere near the top of that last slide.'

The Irish kids were in the pool when Lee and Will got back in the middle of the afternoon. So were Anna and Ben, the Dutch kids. They all asked where Lee and Will had been.

'At the water park,' Will told them.

'Cool!' Padraig said. 'We went there on our second day. Did you go on the biggest slide – the really steep one?'

'Of course,' Lee said. 'It was a breeze, wasn't it Will.'

'Eh, oh yeah, up we went and then down again. It was like a little kids' slide in the park.'

'That's right. I hardly even noticed I was going down it. It was a doddle. We enjoyed it so much that we wanted to do it several more times, except that the queue was incredibly long by the time we got there, so we couldn't.'

Padraig was suitably – if gullably – impressed.

'No sign of the Perfect Family?' Will asked.

'Nope. Haven't shown up all day.'

Anna asked what they were talking about and Carmel explained. 'I guess they're off spending their millions somewhere else today,' she concluded.

'This could be our big chance,' Lee said. 'If they're away we might be able to get into their room.'

'But wouldn't that be breaking and entering,' Carmel said. 'Which would be illegal.'

'Well, only a little bit illegal,' Lee said.

'Or not illegal at all if the door was opened to us,' Will said thoughtfully. He had an idea.

'Do you honestly think you'll get away with it?' Anna asked after Will had explained his idea.

Will shrugged. 'What's the worst that can happen?'

'Maybe they will call the police, no?'

'I doubt it. They're more likely just to chase us away.'

'Perhaps. I'm not sure.'

'Oh, come on,' Padraig said, 'it'll be a laugh. I'm up for it.'

'Good,' Will said. 'What about the rest of you?'

The rest said they were too, even Anna, though she clearly wasn't convinced. Ben sniggered when she explained it to him.

'Okay, we might as well do it now. And if there's no one in we'll just have to come back later.

They all headed off to collect what they needed, then met again in Reception half an hour later. This time they were able to take the lift to the top of the ten floors. It was a lot easier than the stairs.

'Who's going to do the speaking?' Anna asked.

Everyone pointed at Lee, who was flattered by their confidence in him and, at the same time, nervous about what it meant he was going to have to do.

'You sure?'

They all nodded because they didn't fancy having to do the talking themselves, plus Ben couldn't speak much English anyway.

They walked along the corridor together until they were outside room 1066.

'Okay, let's see them on,' Lee whispered.

Everyone stopped and placed on their head what they had made back in their rooms.

Lee looked at the masks. 'Hmm,' he said, and then, pulling on his own mask, whispered, 'Okay, are you all ready?' Everyone nodded. 'Well, here goes.'

He knocked on the door. After a few moments there was still no answer. He was just turning away and lifting his mask to say it was no use when they all heard the sound of sandals flopping on the hard floor behind the door. Lee quickly pulled his mask back down again.

'Oh, hello children.' It was Mrs Perfect. Lee was dazzled by the pink nail polish on her toes.

The masked brigade of children immediately started singing.

> 'We wish you a Spanish Christmas,
> we wish you a Spanish Christmas,
> we wish you a Spanish Christmas
> and a Happy Summer Holiday.'

'Ah heelo Señora,' Lee said, keeping his voice low and trying his best to mimic the voice of the slimy restaurant owner from their first night in the resort. 'We are weeshing you a happy Spaneesh Christmas.'

'A Spanish Christmas?' the woman said.

'Ah, si, it eez the time for Christmas here in Spain, deeferent from in Breetan. We are singing zee carols for zee holidaymakers. Can we sing wan for you, Señora?'

'Eh, well, how perfectly charming. I suppose …'

'Good, good.' Lee led the others in. All had on masks cut out from the brown carrier bags Will had remembered you were given in the nearby supermarkets. They had coloured them in and drawn faces on them. On Will's instructions, Anna and Ben hadn't cut the tops off their bags, they'd just cut eye, nose and mouth holes because of their blonde hair. Will had reminded them that there weren't too many natural golden blondes in Spain.

The group of carol singers shuffled through the door and, to their surprise, entered a room exactly like the ones they were all staying in. Lee looked around for signs of wealth and opulence, but there weren't too many to be seen, not unless you counted a single bottle of wine.

It seemed that Perfect Mother and Perfect Father had only just awoken from an afternoon snooze. Lee thought this was good news because they ought to still be a bit dopey, like his sister used to be after she woke up; and, for that matter, like Lee himself was each morning when he came round from a deep sleep.

Perfect Son and Perfect Daughter were out on the balcony reading, but came inside to see what was happening. Lee tried even harder to disguise his voice. 'Now we are seenging anozer Chreezmass song.'

'Rudolph the red-seeing bullock
Had a very shiny nose,
And if you ever saw it
You would even say it glows.

All of the angry matadors
Laughed at him and called him names.
They always made poor Rudolph
Join in all their matador games.'

Mr and Mrs Perfect were stunned into silence by this performance, as were Perfect Son and Perfect Daughter.

'Dat eez us,' Lee said, keen to get out as fast as possible.

'Oh right. Well that was very, eh, well …'

'Interesting,' said Mr Perfect. 'Very interesting. I had no idea that Christmas came to Spain in the middle of summer.'

'Eet eez a new theeng from the European Union in Brussels.'

'Eh, right. I certainly hadn't heard about that.'

'We go now. Cheerio holidaymakers.'

'Ah, well, you must take something for your, eh, excellent singing,' Mrs Perfect said, keen to be remembered as a perfect hostess and perfect holidaymaker abroad, unlike the riff-raff that usually let the side down.

'No, no,' Lee said. 'Eez not necessary.'

'Oh, but I insist!' Mrs Perfect skuttled about the apartment trying to find something.

'Charlotte … Charles … quick, bring me that box of chocolates you had earlier.'

'Oh but do we have to, Mother?' Charlotte asked demurely.

'Of course, Darling. These traditional and authentic Spanish children have gone to great lengths to entertain us with their, eh …' 'Interesting,' Mr Perfect added again. 'That's right, Charlotte, Dear, their interesting singing. It's only proper and decent that one rewards their sterling efforts.'

Charlotte and Charlie silently handed over their box of chocolates to their mother, who in turn handed them to Lee. 'There you go. And I hope you have a lovely Spanish Christmas.'

'Grassy ass, Señora.'

Lee backed out faster than a naked man reversing

away from a bee hive. The others backed out with him.

'Bye!' Mrs Perfect called as she shut the door gently behind them.

Lee didn't run down the corridor immediately. He stood outside the door and listened to the voices inside. *Then* he ran with the others.

'What is it?' Padraig asked.

'Yes, what has happened?' Anna said.

Lee got his breath back now that they were in the lift heading down.

'I think Mr Perfect just woke up properly. That stuff about the European Union having moved the Spanish Christmas? Well,' and Lee looked sternly at Will as he said this, 'it suddenly dawned on him that it was a complete load of nonsense. Spain has been celebrating Christmas at exactly the same time of year as us for … well, forever! And the European Union isn't about to change that.'

'It was only an idea,' Will said, miffed at the criticism.

'Well it worked for so long as we were inside their apartment,' Carmel said.

'Yeah, and what a rubbish apartment,' Paula commented. 'It's no better than ours. *And* you have to go all the way to the top floor in the lift to get to it.'

'It wasn't at all what I expected,' Lee admitted.

'It was not so smart,' Anna said, and Ben nodded in agreement.

'I didn't see any jewels or butlers or anything,' Paula complained.

'No, but we've got these Belgian chocolates,' Lee said, lifting the lid. 'And that's something. We tricked them and that's the main thing. We've shown how stupid they are.'

'But look!'

'The gluttons!'

'I don't believe it,' Will said.

'Oh Lads!' Padraig cried. 'There's only three chocolates left!'

'They've eaten the whole lot! No wonder they're all
so podgy.'

Lee ripped up his mask in frustration. 'How miserly
can you get. Three chocolates between …' He counted
quickly. 'Between seven of us. Not even half a chocolate each.'

'But it wasn't the point to get chocolates,' Anna
pointed out.

'No, but it would have been nice,' Lee retorted.
'Especially after all the hard work we put in to make
our masks.'

'They're only brown bags over our heads,' Anna
said.

'Anna's right,' Carmel agreed. 'It wasn't like we put a
lot of effort into the designs.'

'We'll need to get them some other way,' Will declared.
'We can't let them get away with this.'

'Oh we won't,' Lee told them all. 'We won't.'

DAY FIVE

Creepy Kev was doing the mid-morning rounds at the poolside. He could be heard some distance away interrogating guests who were with his holiday company.

'Things going alright for you, yeah? Heh heh heh. You want to go on any more trips, heh heh heh?'

'Oh no, somebody save us!' Lee's dad begged as Creepy Kev moved closer to them. 'That lad has a voice like machine-gun fire. I feel as if I'm in a war zone.'

'Let's all go in swimming,' Will suggested.

'Yeah!' Rebecca cried.

Lee had a better idea. 'Rebecca, why don't you attack Creepy Kev the way you attack any friends of mine who ever come to the house? Then maybe he won't come and annoy us.'

He hadn't meant it seriously, but Rebecca hadn't realised that and headed off in Creepy Kev's direction. When she reached him she slapped one of the scrawny legs sticking out from below his not-very-well-ironed shorts.

'Aow! What was that …?' He looked down. 'Oh, it's you, eh …'

'Rebecca,' she told him.

'Yes, heh heh heh.'

'Why do you keep saying that?'

'Saying what?'

'Heh heh heh.'

'Oh, do I?'

'Yes.'

'Heh heh heh.'

'See, you just did it again.'

Creepy Kev tried to ignore her now and continued along the rows of sunloungers, searching out new prey. But Rebecca followed. 'My brother calls you Creepy Kev,' she said.

'Oh no,' moaned Lee, who had heard her say this. He was lying on a sunlounger and pulled the peak of his cap down over his face in the hope that he wouldn't be recognised.

'He can't do anything,' Will whispered. 'You're a guest of his company. What can he say?'

'Heh heh heh?' Lee suggested. 'It's what he normally says about everything. Kevin, your granny's seriously ill and has been rushed to hospital. "Heh heh heh." Kevin, your pet cat's been flattened under a steamroller. "Heh heh heh." I honestly don't think anything or anyone could make him say anything else. It's a habit – a bad one, like smoking.'

Rebecca wasn't prepared to be so readily dismissed by Creepy Kev. She followed him to his next group.

'Hi, there,' Creepy Kev said to the guests. 'You probably remember me, heh heh heh.'

'Oh yes, how could we forget,' a man said, forced to lay down a paperback book he was reading.

'Just checking to see if you want to come on any more of our fantastic trips. A cruise … a beach night followed by an authentic and traditional Spanish meal ….'

Rebecca interrupted. 'Do you get paid for selling the trips?' she asked. 'Are you a salesman?' One of her dad's friends was a salesman, so she knew what it meant.

'Eh …'

'Good question,' the man said. 'Do you?'

'Well, not really …'

'So yes?'

'Heh heh heh. Well a little bit, I suppose.'

The man turned to Rebecca. 'You'll go far, Young Lady.'

Creepy Kev looked as if he wished Rebecca would go far. The further the better.

'No thanks,' the holidaymaker said, leaving Creepy Kev to move on without success.

Lee decided that going swimming would be the best thing after all and dived in while Creepy Kev's back was turned.

Padraig was already in the pool trying to see how far he could swim underwater. He could almost manage a breadth.

'That's impressive,' Lee told him.

'I need to be able to hold my breath,' Padraig said.

'Why's that?'

'For when my da farts. He absolutely honks the place out sometimes. It's as if a truck full of rotting sewage has been poured down our chimney. The worst is when he has a curry. He wipes out most of the ozone layer when he lets rip after a plate of tikka massala.'

Lee knew from personal experience the effect a curry could have, and so sympathised.

'What are you doing today?' Lee asked.

'My ma and da want to go down to the beach – for a change of scenery – so we'll be going down, too.'

The idea of playing in the sand and sea appealed to Lee. 'Maybe I could persuade my lot to go as well.'

'You should. All the adults could talk to each other, and that way they wouldn't need to go bothering us.'

'I'll ask them.'

Creepy Kev had gone back inside the hotel, so it was safe to get out of the pool again. Dripping wet, Lee went over to try and convince his family and Will that what they really wanted to do was pick up all their gear and head down to the beach.

Lee succeeded.

The adults introduced themselves to each other on the way down. It turned out that Carmel, Padraig and Paula's 'da' also did something to do with farming, so he and Uncle Raymond were soon deep in conversation, with Lee's dad listening in. The kids' 'ma' was soon talking to Lee's mum about the kids – how they were enjoying themselves, how they were growing up so fast and all that other nonsense parents, especially mums, are always getting engrossed in.

The beach was busy, but they were lucky. As they arrived, another group were packing up to go and they were able to take their spot.

Lee was still conscious of having scared all the swimmers from the sea shortly after having arrived, but no one said anything, so either they'd forgotten all about it or no longer recognised him because of the slight tan he'd developed.

Will persuaded Rebecca that the rest of them should bury her in the sand, so she sat down while the others scooped up bucketfuls to cover her legs with. A few minutes later, by which time she was buried up to her chest, she was unable to move because of the weight of the sand.

'Let me out,' she told them. Carmel moved forward to help release her, but Lee stopped her. 'Hang on,' he said, then turned to Rebecca. 'Now, Rebecca. If you want out you have to promise to never again attack any of my friends when they come to the house, okay?'

Rebecca just grinned, proud of striking fear into the hearts of Lee's friends.

'I mean it,' Lee warned. 'No more attacks.'

More grins.

'Okay, let's all go down to the sea,' Lee said, turning around and encouraging the others to do the same. 'We'll just leave Rebecca here at the mercy of the tide.

Oh, and the giant sand worms.'

'What giant sand worms?' Paula asked, concerned.

'The ones that slide under the sand really quickly and then snap up anything alive that's sticking down underneath it. They're quite big – say about the size of a python.'

'They're enormous,' Padraig informed everyone. 'And they can eat you whole.'

'Let me out!' Rebecca hollered.

'Do you promise?' Lee asked.

'No,' Rebecca said defiantly.

'Oh well then …' Lee started walking down the beach.

'Let me out!' Rebecca called again, more urgently this time.

'Do you promise?' Lee asked again.

'Okay,' Rebecca agreed. 'I promise.'

'Good.' Lee returned to the pile of sand and scraped enough off to allow Rebecca to free herself.

As soon as she was on her feet she started attacking Lee. 'Hoy!' he said. 'You promised.'

'I only promised not to attack your friends,' Rebecca told him. 'I didn't say I wouldn't attack *you*.'

Lee sprinted down the beach to escape his enraged little sister.

Some big waves were breaking just short of the shore, where a line of people had gathered who, it seemed, wanted to be sent flying by the sea's power. They were mad, those people, sitting targets for the waves. So Lee, Will and the Irish kids joined them and were duly knocked off their feet.

'There aren't any jellyfish in here, are there?' Will asked quietly, learning from Lee's previous beach-clearing mistake.

Lee picked himself up after being bowled over again. 'There must be some, I suppose.'

'But not the killers – the man-o'-wars with their deadly tentacles.'

'I sure hope not.'

It was tiring constantly having to pick yourself up, and after a while they decided to head back up the beach. They were passing through a quiet area halfway back to where their parents were sitting when Padraig said, 'Look!' The others all followed his finger (even though it was rude to point) and saw … The Perfect Family. They were tucked in behind a hideously old-fashioned (as opposed to traditional and authentic) windbreak. Even a blind man couldn't have missed the red-, orange- and yellow-striped material sticking out of the sand on four aluminium poles. Presumably they'd erected it as much so they didn't have to associate with other people as to keep off the non-existent breeze.

The minds of all five of them started racing. What could they do to bring the snobs down a peg or two and pay back Perfect Daughter and Perfect Son for having eaten all but three of the chocolates in the box they'd handed over for the carol singing? None of them had any immediate ideas, but they were thinking hard. Then Padraig said, 'Maybe they'll go swimming and we can nick all their stuff.'

'We can't just steal it,' Carmel said. 'That wouldn't be very nice.'

'*They're* not very nice,' Padraig responded.

'Even so, that still doesn't excuse stealing.'

'I've got a better idea,' Lee said. 'Come on.'

He led them back to where their parents were sitting, picked up all the buckets and spades they'd brought with them and headed off again, back down to the water's edge.

'What are we going to do?' little Paula asked, excited.

'Fill these up with water,' Lee said, handing out the buckets, 'and you'll see.'

They did as he asked and walked back up the beach, being careful to spill as little of the water as possible. Lee plonked himself down on an empty piece of hot sand ten metres away from the back of the Perfect's windbreak.

'Right, pretend we're all making sandcastles,' Lee said. 'And make sure you're all facing up the beach, away from the sea and away from the Perfects.'

They all sat down and started moving the sand around, digging a moat around an imaginary castle. (They would have built a real one but the sand was too dry for the grains to stick together.)

'That's fine,' Lee said after a few minutes. 'Now remember, keep facing up the beach. Don't turn round, whatever happens. And make it seem as if we're all still playing in the sand.

Lee lifted one of the buckets of water and placed it in front of him. Then he took a spade, dipped it in, and loaded it.

Will caught on and did the same. So did Padraig.

'Nice and high,' Lee said. 'So they think it's raining.'

All three lined themselves up, looking over their shoulders to make sure they would hit their target.

Lee whispered, 'Three, two, one ...'

They let fly, flicking the watery contents of their spades over their heads and watching it soar up and over the Perfect Family's ghastly windbreak. Before it landed they buried their spades in sand and made it look as if they were just playing normally.

'Hoy!' a voice called. 'What was that?' But none of the kids turned around. The sand in front of them was, at that particular moment, the most interesting sand in the whole universe. So absorbing, indeed, that nothing could distract them from it – not even a bemused Mr Perfect standing up and looking out over his windbreak in the hope of working out where the water was coming from.

'I suppose it must have been one of those freak showers,' they heard him tell Mrs Perfect eventually. 'How
frightfully odd.'

'Better a freak shower than a freak show,' Lee whispered. 'Which is what his family is.'

Lee ventured a sneaky look behind him to make sure
Mr Perfect had sat back down, which by now he had,
then unearthed (or unsanded) his spade. 'Again,' he
said.

Another salvo was sent flying over the top of the
windbreak and again the spades were buried immediately. The buckets were all sitting between their legs,
protected by their upper bodies so they couldn't be
seen.

Lee heard the squeak of Mr Perfect's sunlounger as
the toff rolled off it and jumped to his feet even more
quickly this time. 'What the devil's going on! Where's
all that water coming from?'

The five kids pretended to be burying Paula now, just
as they had done earlier with Rebecca. 'More sand!'
Paula said to keep up the illusion. 'More!' The others
duly obliged.

By now Mr Perfect was not only perplexed, but also
irritated. He hated being interrupted when he was trying to read *Top Tips for Toffs* or *Making the Most of Your
Massive Mansion* or whatever was now lying in a heap
on the sand after he'd thrown it aside.

'This is ridiculous!' he said.

'It's not those dreadful seagulls, is it Dear?' Mrs Perfect was heard asking. 'You remember what they did to
the car that time after it had just been valeted.'

'No, no. It's definitely water.'

'Bury me deeper!' Paula was still urging the others,
covering for them.

Once again Mr Perfect was at a loss to understand

what was happening, and he sat down.

'Let's do something different,' Padraig said. 'Come on, bring your buckets. But we'll need to be fast getting away.'

Padraig slid down the sand until the windbreak was right next to him, on the downward slope. He raised his fingers for a silent countdown. Three … two … one … All three of them turned their buckets upside down, then scrambled back, scooping sand into the buckets as they went and covering over the few tell-tale drips caused by water sloshing out of their buckets as they'd moved in for the attack.

From the safety of where Paula was buried they watched for a moment. Some of the water sank harmlessly into the sand, but most of it ran under the bottom of the windbreak.

There was a longer delay than when they'd fired water over the top, but just as they were starting to worry that their plan hadn't worked …

'Agghh. We're being flooded out!' It was Mrs Perfect this time. 'Look! My copy of this month's *Very Expensive Things to Spend Your Millions On*! It's ruined!'

'Right, what's going on?' Mr Perfect demanded angrily.

Lee, Will, Carmel, Padraig and Paula were a picture of innocence, taking simple pleasure in the pure, golden sand, which was all they needed to entertain themselves. No modern games or gadgets, just good old-fashioned, isn't-it-wonderful-to-see-children-making-their-own-entertainment-instead-of-relying-on-adults-to-serve-it-up-on-a-plate amusement. How could anyone be suspicious of them? How could anyone possibly suspect that they might fire water over the Perfect Family's windbreak or try to flood their precious spot on the beach?

It seemed that grumpy Mr Perfect could.

'You lot!' he called. 'What's going on?'

Only Carmel turned round, as they'd agreed. It was best to use a girl, because girls were generally thought by gullible adults to be more blameless, righteous and responsible. Carmel rustled up her best *Who? Us?* expression, looking around her as if Mr Perfect was surely speaking to someone else. 'What's going on with what?' she replied.

'Have you been throwing water at us and letting it run under our windbreak?'

Lee and Will were particularly keen not to show their faces given the ticking off Mr Perfect had given them at the swimming pool earlier in the week. He would no doubt recognise them and assume that they were to blame. As if! And Paula tried to distract him by calling, 'More!' again, even though she was, by now, nearly up to her neck in sand.

However, Mr Perfect was a man on a mission – a mission to find out who was soaking his family, which was why he said, 'Some oaf's been soaking me and my family, and I want to know who.'

'Well it certainly wasn't *me*,' Carmel said indignantly. Which was true, strictly speaking.

'I'm not saying it was you,' Mr Perfect said.

'Well it sounded like you were. It sounded like you were accusing me of doing it. I'm going to tell my da' about the accusations you're making, accusing an innocent girl like me of doing something like that.' Carmel stood up and made as if she was about to storm off up the beach. It was a brilliant move, one Lee, Will and Padraig hadn't been expecting her to make. She had called Mr Perfect's bluff perfectly.

'Well now, okay, there really isn't any need for that, Young Lady. Just keep an eye out for any hooligans, will you? They're terrorising normal people like us.'

'Okay, I will do,' Carmel agreed, sitting back down

as Mr Perfect disappeared back behind his windbreak, mumbling to himself about how the children of today had no manners and how this sort of thing wouldn't have happened back in his day.

'Eh, that's enough, now,' Paula said, spitting sand out of her mouth because the boys hadn't wanted to stop while Mr Perfect was there and had now buried her to slightly past her chin.

Throughout Carmel's exchange with Mr Perfect the three boys had found it incredibly difficult not to snigger or laugh out loud. Now, as Paula broke free from the sand, they were able to let themselves go with a genuine reason. Mr Perfect's head appeared above the windbreak momentarily but disappeared again when he saw that it was simply the buried child wriggling out from under all that sand.

Paula said. 'Is it lunchtime yet? I'm hungry.'

Padraig volunteered to run over and ask. He was back a minute later, excited.

'What is it? Are we going somewhere special?'

'No. I've had a brilliant idea.' He revealed a handful of string he'd picked up off the beach, then started whispering, from which the others gathered that he had a brilliantly sneaky idea. And they were correct. It was the sort of sneaky idea Lee was used to coming up with, so he was able to admire Padraig's similar cunning.

Five minutes later, Lee, Will, Carmel and Paula set off up the beach towards where their parents were sitting. They didn't go far, though, because they wanted to see Padraig's plan executed.

The four of them sat down and looked back to where Padraig was buried in sand, just where Paula had been. They waved, but of course he couldn't wave back. Instead, he grinned.

A moment later the Perfect Family's windbreak suddenly collapsed in a heap, giving Mrs Perfect such a fright that she fell off her sunlounger and landed on a tube of sun cream that was lying open beside her, squirting a big blob through the air and onto Perfect Daughter's perfectly platted hair. Everyone on the beach stopped what they were doing (even if they were doing nothing) to stare as Perfect Daughter screamed loudly, thinking the white goo was from one of those gulls Perfect Mother had mentioned earlier. Her scream caused Perfect Son to drop the can of juice he was drinking. It emptied itself out onto his stomach, from where it headed downwards, so that when he, too, leapt up, it looked as if he'd failed to make it to the toilet (or the sea – it's really the same thing if you're on the beach) in time.

Throughout this commotion, Padraig sat perfectly still, marooned in the sand. The only clue to his involvement was a very slight shifting of the sand around his left hand – a hand that had string tied around it – where he'd given a short, sharp tug a moment earlier. That had caused the other end of the line, all of which was buried under a dusting of sand, to tighten; and as it had been tied around the middle pole of the hideous windbreak ....

Lee, Will, Carmel and Paula fell about laughing. Mr Perfect stared at them, but they were so far away that they couldn't possibly have had anything to do with the collapse.

The furious Mr Perfect stomped around the beach. His face was purple with rage, and, because he couldn't see anyone to blame, he looked as if he might explode with frustration.

Lee thought his sides were going to split open, he was laughing so much. He hoped not, because it would be very messy, plus he'd get sand all over his insides, which would be uncomfortable.

Lee's dad wandered down to where they were rolling

about laughing.

'What's going on?' he asked brightly, pleased to see all the children so happy.

'The Perfects' windshield fell over,' Lee managed to force out in between laughs.

'Oh, right. How did that happen?'

They all shrugged their shoulders. 'No idea.'

Padraig had decided that sufficient time had elapsed for him to be able to make a getaway without drawing too much suspicion to himself. As he shook free from the sand, Lee frantically pointed to his wrist, reminding Padraig to remove the string before walking off, otherwise the whole windshield would follow him.

It was too hot to sit out in the middle of the day. While the Irish family went back to the hotel, Lee, Will and Lee's family went for lunch in the shade at one of the beachfront restaurants, where Lee's dad explained the plan for that evening.

'There's a show on tonight,' he said.

'Brilliant!' Lee enthused.

'Yes, the holiday reps are putting it on.'

'Aw.' Lee's delight drained away like water down a particularly wide plughole. 'It'll be rubbish in that case.'

'I'm sure it'll be fine,' his mum said. 'They'll do their best.'

'But look at them,' Lee told her. 'A witch, a creep and a girl who speaks like Darth Vader and who dad can't keep his eyes off.'

'Or his hands, sometimes,' his mum noted. 'Still, they're also running a talent competition.'

'Do the losers have to become holiday reps?' Will asked. 'It would certainly explain the ones we've got.'

'You should all go in for it,' Uncle Raymond said.

'Doing what?' Lee asked.

'Well, from what I hear, you've got a real talent for causing trouble.'

Lee and Will groaned at this terrible joke. 'Well if that's the standard of the comedians then we've nothing to fear,' Lee told him.

'Have a think about it,' Lee's mum encouraged. 'According to the posters, you could win a fantastic prize.'

'Yeah,' Lee said. 'What's that? A chance to leave the show early?'

'Don't be such a cynic,' his dad told him. Lee didn't know he was being one, because he didn't know what a cynic was.

'We'll need to think about doing some shopping before then,' Lee's mum said. 'We need to get some presents to take back with us.'

'Tacky souvenir stuff, you mean,' Lee said.

'No. Nice presents. For your grandparents.'

'Hmm.'

'And no doubt you'll want to get something for your parents, won't you, Will?'

'Eh, yeah. I was just thinking that. Maybe a CD of some traditional and authentic Spanish music.'

Lee shook his head. 'No, you don't want to get them that.'

'Why not?'

'In case they actually play it. Then you'd have to suffer it, too.'

'Good point.'

'I'm sure we'll find something,' Lee's mum said. 'And we might as well do it this afternoon, that way we won't have to spoil our last day with it.'

That was a depressing thought. Five nights had already passed and this would be their sixth. One more full day left before they'd have to head home.

'I don't want to go home,' Rebecca said. 'I like it here.'

'We all do, Dear,' Lee's mum told her. 'But we've only paid for a week.'

Rebecca made a miserable face.

'Well, that was boring,' Lee said as they arrived back at the hotel after finishing their shopping. No one disagreed. 'And talking of boring, only a few hours until the reps' show starts.'

It was hot enough to fry an egg on your stomach. Uncle Raymond had even offered to prove it. Yet some people seemed to love sweating like a runner in the desert when the sun was at its highest. Lee couldn't understand them.

Lee's mum and dad decided to go for a sleep indoors, out of the sun. Uncle Raymond said he would stay by the pool and keep an eye on Rebecca. Lee and Will decided to go for a wander around the hotel grounds, hoping to catch up with the Dutch or Irish kids.

'But first I'm going to sit in the shade for a bit,' Lee declared.

Will knew where Lee's favourite shady spot was, so he headed to the toilet, saying he would join Lee in a minute … if he didn't decide to have one more go on the Space Invaders machine first … which he probably would.

Lee's favourite piece of shade was beside the lime trees, where a bench sat under a canopy at the end of a side entrance to the hotel. The buildings on either side of the entrance channelled the wind up from the sea, making it much cooler than at the poolside, where the hotel buildings blocked the breeze. No one ever seemed to use the bench, so Lee had claimed it as his own.

He approached it now, climbing down the steps from the back of the hotel.

But Lee stopped before reaching the bottom step and turning the corner. He could hear whispering. Urgent whispering. Serious whispering. He didn't recognise the voice, but from the reflection on the side of a large window he was able to see its owner's outline. And he was shocked.

'Ladies and Gentlemen,' a woman's voice screeched into the darkness. It had to be Angela; it was too witchy to be anyone else's. 'Tonight, live from the hotel's theatre …'

'You mean a room with a curtain hanging down,' Lee mumbled.

'… we present, for your entertainment and enjoyment, the one and only, the fabulous, the amazing and really quite good Reps' Show!'

The announcement was greeted with some gentle, not-very-enthusiastic clapping, as if those present were there only because they felt obliged to be and supposed they'd better be polite.

'And here's your host …' The curtain didn't so much slide back as tear apart and fall to the corners. '… Me!' Angela appeared centre stage.

'Oh what a surprise,' Will grumbled. 'She's come to cast another spell on us.'

Angela was dressed in a sparkly suit and held in front of her a microphone, although no one knew why because, as everyone had experienced at the Welcome Party, her voice was so loud that holidaymakers on other continents could probably hear her.

'Is everybody happy?' she asked, brimming with enthusiasm. In response a few people mouthed: 'I sup-

Spooky Samantha turned to the audience for help. 'Oh yes I am,' she called, with minimal backing.

And so unfolded a story of a fight for the right to be the hotel's ghost. Who would win, the supernatural sheet-over-the-head Kev or the chain-smoking, chain-toting spectral Samantha? How many guests would be scared witless before the battle ended? And would the two ghouls get much-needed sun tans if they hung around the pool area a bit more?

It got worse: they introduced music. On the upside, Creepy Kev and Spooky Samantha didn't have to sing because the music was so loud that any ghosts who had been foolish enough to take up residence in the Hotel del Sol would have been scared off instantly.

The story ended after one song, with the two ghosts agreeing to share the hotel because there were more than enough guests to go round if ever they felt like scaring a few folk.

Ample Angela came back on stage and her voice came back into everyone's eardrums (not that it had really left them in the first place). 'And now, as a special treat, our three fabulous bar staff – Tia Maria, Mora Drinka and Neva Againa – will entertain you with some amazing juggling!'

The three girls nervously took to the stage. They each carried a couple of silver cocktail shakers and were soon tossing them into the air and then back and forth between each other. Fortunately they all had day jobs, because they would need them to pay for the repairs to the cocktail shakers, which they dropped with alarming regularity. If they were waiting for a phone call from the circus then their wait was going to be a long one.

Despite their poor performance, everyone gave the Spanish girls a hearty round of applause, mainly because it put off whatever was coming next, which was bound to be even worse than what had gone before.

Angela was still portraying boundless enthusiasm for the show. 'Now we're going to have a short break, but then we'll get on with the part of the show where *you* get the chance to take part and showcase *your* talents!'

'Oh joy,' Lee's dad groaned.

'Every one of you must have some sort of special talent, whether it be playing tunes on your cheeks – either pair of them – singing a song or break-dancing, so come on up and share it with your fellow guests …'

'Inmates, more like,' Uncle Raymond muttered.

'… because there are fabulous prizes on offer to the winners! And it doesn't matter how young or old you are, all we want is to enjoy your special abilities!'

There was a buzz of anticipation in the audience. Perhaps someone had found a trapdoor through which everyone could escape.

But no, it seemed some people actually *wanted* to take part. More particularly, they wanted to inflict themselves on the rest of the audience.

'Okay, well I'm pleased to say that we have a raft of entrants!' Angela announced after several people had ventured forward to add their names to the list of people wanting to appear and torture their fellow holiday-makers. 'If I had a raft of entrants,' Lee's dad said, 'I'd tow them out to a very deep part of the sea – say, right above the Mariana Trench, which is eleven miles deep – then leave them there without any paddles to get back with.'

'So I'll see you all after the break!'

'Excuse me, I need to go to the toilet,' Lee said as Angela left the stage.

Will felt a hefty nudge in his side from Lee's elbow. 'Oh, eh, I think I'd better go too,' he said. 'It could be a while until we get another chance.'

The two boys stood and squeezed past Lee's dad's

long legs.

'I thought only girls always went to the toilet in pairs,' Uncle Raymond observed as they departed.

Lee and Will kept their heads down and didn't say anything as they headed for the door.

As soon as the two boys were outside, Will grabbed Lee's arm. 'What's this all about? What's the big secret? Why did you want me to come out to the toilet with you?'

'So I could tell you what's going on. I couldn't tell you earlier because mum and dad were around.'

'So what *is* going on?'

'Have you noticed anyone missing from the rep show?'

'Eh … people who can act?'

'I'm being serious. Think. Who's here in the hotel but not in the audience?'

'I would think there must be quite a few people. Anyone with any common sense, I'd say, given how bad the show has been so far. So how about giving me a clue?'

'Okay. Posh.'

'Oh, you mean The Perfects.'

Lee nodded. 'Exactly.'

'Well that's not much of a surprise. I can't imagine this being their sort of thing. They're probably away to a night at the opera.'

'No, they're not. I heard them talking earlier; only not in their own voices.'

'Were they any good? They could do impressions in the second half of the show.'

'This was different. They're not really posh at all.'

'What?'

'They've been putting it on all this time. That's not how they really speak.'

Will scratched his head. 'That's weird. Why would anyone pretend to speak like that?'

'I don't know. But they're planning something for to-morrow evening.'

'What?'

'I've no idea, but I reckon they're in league with the Shiny Suits.'

'No way!'

'Think about it. Their bedrooms are next to each other, they've both got fancy cars, they've gone out at the same time …'

'… You've heard them plotting …'

'It makes so much sense.'

Will thought for a moment. 'Lee, you've thought a lot of other things have made sense … and it's turned out that they haven't.'

'A few things, I know. But I'm convinced about this. I heard them mention drugs.'

'Drugs? That's serious.'

'I know.'

'Maybe we shouldn't get involved.'

'Or maybe we should try to save people's lives by rid-ding the world of some stuff that really harms people.'

'And get The Perfects sent to prison.'

'Yeah, that especially. Plenty of people would thank us for that.'

'But what are we going to do?'

Lee was cool and decisive. 'We'll speak to the other kids and see if we can come up with an idea.'

'Where have you two been?' Lee's mum asked as Lee and Will hurried back to their seats.

'Sorry, Mrs Waters,' Will said. 'There was a long queue.'

'Well the show's about to …' Lee's mum began to say before a piercing whine of feedback from the microphone drowned out the rest of her sentence.

'Welcome back, Ladies and Gentlemen,' Angela croaked from the stage. 'It's time to get on with the show again.'

'Oh must we,' Uncle Raymond moaned.

'The sooner it starts the sooner it finishes,' Lee's dad consoled him.

Angela explained what was about to happen and then said, 'And our first contestant is …' Two people stomped their feet on the floor to make up for the fact that there were no drums for a drum roll. '… is John, who's going to sing for us! And what are you going to sing for us, John?' she asked, almost sticking the microphone into his mouth.

'*My Way*,' John announced.

'Oh good,' Lee's mum said. 'That's one of my favourites.'

Not the way John sang it, it wasn't. His singing was dire. He couldn't reach up to the high notes or down to the low ones, but he tried to the very end, which couldn't come soon enough for everyone else. There was a polite round of applause when he finished, mainly because people needed to do something with their hands in the absence of having any tomatoes to throw.

Next up was a little girl called Lucy. She was so young that her mum had to hold her hand while she recited Humpty Dumpty. She was given a round of applause even though she was rubbish, because it's important to encourage children to explore many different career opportunities and Lucy was clearly going to require encouragement to find one that didn't involve getting up on a stage.

'Next, it's Willie McSporran from the Outer Hebrides, and he's going to be doing some impressions!'

Willie got a big hand as he stood up. It hit him on the arm to wish him good luck.

'My first impression is of my dad,' he said. He then said a few things in exactly the same voice as he'd just used for his introduction. His Scottish accent was so strong and melodic that Lee at first thought Willie was singing in Gaelic.

'That's cheating,' Uncle Raymond said. 'How's anyone meant to know what his dad sounds like?!'

'I imagine he's got the accent just perfect,' Lee's mum said.

'Well he would, wouldn't he! They're from the same place!'

'My next impression is of my mum.'

Same accent, only the voice was higher.

'And finally, the prime minister …'

'That's more like it,' Lee's dad said.

'… if he'd been born in the Outer Hebrides.'

Willie obviously thought the prime minister would be exactly the same as his dad, in every respect.

'Fantastic!' Angela bubbled, taking back the microphone. 'Great impressions there from Willie. Maybe one day we'll see him on TV.'

'If so, I'll be changing channels,' Will said. 'He'll probably do an impression of his identical twin brother.'

And so it went on. One person after another climbed on stage – including a man who claimed to look and sound like Elvis Presley but didn't and a woman who, when she 'sang', ended up dueting with most of the neighbourhood's cats – and they were all absolutely dreadful.

'Well, that's our final contender,' Angela announced after what seemed like slightly longer than an eternity.

But Lee wasn't standing for it. He might be a nobody and he might be a bit rubbish at most things, but Lee had decided that it didn't matter any more, he couldn't possibly be any worse than those people who'd stood up there in front of him. Almost without knowing it he rose up from his chair. 'Lee, are you going to the toilet?' his mum asked, but he didn't answer; he was too focused on what he had to do. While Angela was whispering to someone at the side of the stage, trying to work out what she was supposed to do next, Lee approached and said to her, 'Right, *I'll* have a go.'

'Oh, right,' she said. She looked even more like a witch close up. Her face was hairy and she'd put powder on it that only served to emphasise her coat of fur. 'Okay, then.' She turned to the audience. 'A last-minute entrant!' The crowd sighed. Some lost the will to live. 'Please give it up for …' She bent down to Lee. 'What's your name?' 'Lee,' Lee said. 'Please give it up for Lee!'

Lee turned and faced the audience. He had never been on stage before. He'd once tried to get a part in the school play, but the music teacher, The Rat, had only made him first reserve. He froze for a second, nerves getting the better of him. But then he recovered. He had a job to do. He had a mission to achieve. And he had someone to make fun of.

He bent over slightly and, in the same voice that had been tormenting him all holiday said, 'Heh heh heh.'

The audience suddenly woke up. 'The first of our trips is our totally rubbish traditional Spanish mountain fiesta, heh heh heh …' Lee was encouraged by the sight of brightening faces before him. '… for which all monies will be collected by, heh heh heh, our accountant, Fidel. Our driver will take you on a rickety old mini bus up into the mountains where you will be dumped in a restaurant and made to eat horsemeat rolled up in leaves, heh heh heh. Meanwhile, we'll be out the back having a pizza and laughing at all you suckers, heh heh heh!'

The audience loved this. They were rolling around in their seats.

Creepy Kev, on the other hand, was not enjoying this

one bit. He was standing to the side of the stage. At first he glared at Lee. Then, when that didn't have any effect, he started whispering loudly, 'Shut up! Get off!' But Lee knew that for as long as he was on stage there wasn't a thing Creepy Kev could do to stop him.

'And then tonight we'll be treating you to our special Reps' Show, heh heh heh, with traditionally rubbish singing, dodgy dancing and do-it-yourself entertainment, heh heh heh.'

The audience loved Lee's impression of Kev. By making a fool out of their idiot holiday rep who had taken them all for granted and had no idea what they really wanted from their holiday, Lee was doing what they'd all wanted to do throughout the holiday.

Finally, Angela decided to intervene and stepped out in front of Lee, grabbing the microphone from him on her way. 'That was Lee, Ladies and Gentlemen.' For the first time that evening her sentence didn't have an exclamation mark at the end of it.

Lee, who was standing behind her, did a quick impression of a witch on a broomstick, without Angela seeing him, and found that the audience knew exactly what he was meaning. They rewarded him with another round of applause.

The winner of the talent competition was to be decided by the volume of cheering, but no one else stood a chance, because by this time several people (Uncle Raymond, Will and Rebecca included) were chanting 'Come on Lee-ee! Come on Lee-ee!' and more and more others were joining in. Angela could barely make herself heard above the noise. 'I take it you think Lee should be the winner?' she suggested. Everyone cheered and banged on their tables. 'Well, okay, then.'

Lee, who had stepped down from the stage, had to step back up onto it again to receive his prize. He hadn't expected this and hurriedly tried to compose his acceptance speech in his head. He'd seen actors do it for Oscars so he knew roughly how it was supposed to go.

Unluckily for Creepy Kev, it was his job to hand over the prize. At the back of the stage he shook his head and pleaded with Angela, but she wasn't letting him off the hook. He plodded miserably onto the stage, with everyone shouting 'heh heh heh' and thinking it was incredibly funny.

'Here you go,' was as much congratulations as Creepy Kev could muster as he held out his hand.

'There's nothing there,' Lee pointed out to him.

'Oh? It's an invisible pen. Can't you see it?'

'Just because you're an idiot doesn't mean I'm one, too,' Lee told him, forcing Creepy Kev to bring out an envelope from his pocket.

'What is it?' Lee asked. 'A hundred euros? Free tickets for the water park?'

'It's twenty euros.'

'Twenty! Is that all?! What a rubbish prize.'

The audience agreed. 'Rubbish! Rubbish!' they began chanting.

'Eh, well, heh heh heh, maybe we could make that fifty euros.'

'A hundred,' Lee said.

'Eighty.'

'A hundred.'

'Okay, then. A hundred.'

'Nice haggling with you,' Lee said.

Lee snatched the microphone from Creepy Kev and turned to the audience. 'Thanks very much, everyone. Before I go, I'd just like to say a few words of thanks. First, to my mum and dad for bringing us here – I never could have made it this far without you. Second, to my friend Will, my sister and my Uncle Raymond for their undying support. Also, to my grannies back home who can still touch their bums with their feet: cheers for the amusement.' Lee demonstrated how they did this. 'Then, there's the doctors who once saved my life and without whom I wouldn't be here. Plus, there's …'

Angela intervened. 'Yes, and anyone else who knows you,' she finished off for him. 'Well done, Lee.'

The boy wonder took a bow, then another, then another. Then Angela gave him a nudge with her hip that sent him stumbling towards the side of the stage and back to where his family and Will were waiting to welcome home a new star. This week some crummy rep show, next week a prime-time slot on television. It could be the start of a whole new career. The kid who, once, nobody knew and even fewer wanted to know, would be an international superstar rubbing shoulders with the rich and famous, and impersonating many of them. Of course, there'd be loads of fan mail to deal with, but he could always hire someone to take care of that because he'd be loaded.

DAY SIX

When he went down to the pool the next day, Lee fully expected everyone to point at him, saying, 'That's the superstar boy wonder from last night.' But how quickly the world moved on. Famous one day, forgotten the next. No wonder movie stars and singers were always looking to get their pictures in the paper by pretending to have new (or, indeed, several) girlfriends or boyfriends so the media would notice them and the public would remember who they were. It was an important lesson to learn. Lee had heard an actor being interviewed who'd said, 'You're only as good as your last movie,' and now he understood what it meant. Last night Lee had been this week's winner, this morning he was Mr Nobody again, just a normal kid from a normal family on a normal summer holiday.

Anyway, there was no time to dwell on his success the previous night. He and Will needed to think ahead to the coming evening.

Will had suggested that they tell Lee's mum and dad about their suspicions, but Lee had said that they would only tell them to stay well away and keep out of trouble and what fun would that be? Then Will suggested telling Uncle Raymond, on the basis that he was 'always up for stuff'.

Lee reckoned this was a much better idea. Will was right, Uncle Raymond was always up for taking chances and doing things that more sensible adults would think were a bit dodgy.

However, that would need to wait until later because Uncle Raymond was lying next to Lee's mum and dad, so the two boys set off to see if they could find the other kids.

The Irish kids were easy to find. They were in their usual spot on the beach.

'Hey, Lads,' Padraig greeted them. 'How's things?'

'Things are … well, actually, that's what we've come to talk to you about …'

Lee's dad decided it was important to concentrate on getting the most out of the remaining hours of their holiday and announced that he was going windsurfing that afternoon. It would be his active treat. Everyone else said they'd go down to the beach with him – so they could laugh if he repeatedly fell off the board and into the sea (unless, of course, they saw the fin of a killer whale or a shark sticking out of the water nearby, in which case they'd shout very very very loudly for him to get out of the water – pronto).

It was difficult not to count down every minute of the last day, but if you did, that was all you'd have done – count – and you did that every day in school, during maths, so what was the point of that. No, you somehow had to forget about it being the last day, treat it like any other, and live it to the full and go to bed feeling as if you'd got the most out of it.

The Irish kids joined them back at the pool half an hour later. They splashed about together, diving for items they dropped to the bottom of the pool's shallow end. Rebecca loved having older kids to play with and Carmel and Paula paid her lots of attention, which she loved even more, and even Padraig did his best to include her in their games, letting her catch the ball sometimes when they were playing piggy in the middle.

The reps appeared about lunchtime, doing their rounds and reminding everyone of their flight times for the next morning. Creepy Kev went nowhere near Lee's family, leaving that to Sexy Samantha, which was fine by the Irish kids' dad, as well as Lee's. A quiet 'heh heh heh' rose from the pool as Creepy Kev moved from group to group, but Lee ignored it, certain that Creepy Kev was saying it less often now. Really he'd done him a favour by taking the mickey out of him on stage and making him self-conscious about saying heh heh heh all the time; at least, that's what Lee decided.

Lunchtime came around all too quickly (whereas at school, lunchtime – and the hot dogs it meant Lee would eat – didn't come quickly enough) and then it was the afternoon. Just before three o'clock they all headed off to the beach to watch Lee's dad making a fool of himself windsurfing.

All week they'd seen some fantastic windsurfers skimming the waves as they tore across the bay at great speed, harnessing the wind to power them along. They wore fancy gear, multi-coloured like the cyclists in the Tour de France, that was meant to keep them dry and warm, except that they never seemed to fall in. Then there was Lee's dad: plain red shorts and red skin, nervously entering the water and trying to get onto his board. He rocked from side to side, then fell in. He climbed aboard again, steadied himself and pulled on a knotted rope to lift the sail, first taking it sideways to get rid of the water that made it too heavy to raise straight up. Next, he tried to find the wind. But it found him first, and over he went, the sail coming down on top of him. He swam out from underneath it, waved to those laughing on the shore and heaved himself back up for another attempt. Again he lifted the sail, only this time he had a better idea of what to expect and turned the sail so that the wind filled it and sent him on his way. For ten metres. Then he fell in again.

But as the hour for which he'd hired the board progressed he persevered, and as a result he improved to such an extent that he almost made it across the bay without falling off. It was just a pity that at one stage he didn't know how to turn the board around and sail back; instead, he had to drag it along near the shore, excusing himself as he disturbed swimmers and those playing in the waves.

He joined his family where they were sitting on their beach towels. 'Man, that was hard work,' he said. 'I'm cream crackered. I feel as if I've taken part in a day-long tug-of-war session.' He collapsed in a heap on his towel, only to discover that it was covering a large pit that Lee and Rebecca had dug while he'd been wind-surfing. He fell in, bum first, leaving his legs and arms flailing above the sand. Uncle Raymond and Lee's mum thought this was hilarious and Lee almost wet himself laughing.

While they were away, Lee's dad bought everyone a slice of melon from a youth who'd come wandering along the beach with a coolbox full of them.

'Oh well, it's only right that we have a laugh today, because tomorrow morning we'll be on the flight home,' Uncle Raymond said. 'Back to reality and back to work.'

'Not for us,' Lee reminded him.

'Yes, I know. It's alright for you kids, isn't it, with your umpteen weeks of holiday.' He looked at his watch, brushing some sand off the face.

They got up, pulled their shorts out to release the build-up of sand that had somehow found its way into every nook and cranny, and headed back up the beach to the hotel as the sun sank slowly on their last afternoon.

In fact the sun wasn't sinking *slowly*, it was diving as if there were gold somewhere just below the horizon, and in its place appeared a stack of clouds of the big, dark, we're-comin'-to-get-you variety, the variety that tends to end up chucking several thousands of gallons of water on your head.

Lee's family weren't the only ones who'd noticed the sudden appearance of the clouds; everyone else had, too, and there was an instant mass exodus from the beach. It was as if someone had set up a stall on the promenade giving out free ice-creams (which sadly they hadn't). Cafés, bars and restaurants that had been empty all afternoon suddenly filled to the brim with sunbathers anxious not to have their tans washed off in a downpour.

There were a few 'oohs' when the clouds burst open, then a few 'ahhs' as the rain started pelting down, and then a lot of comments like 'Oh man, that went right down the back of my neck' and 'Hey, how come I'm getting drenched through this ceiling?' as more and more roofs failed to cope with the deluge.

'It'll just be a passing summer shower,' Lee's mum said.

It was a statement she was regretting three quarters of an hour later when the rain was still plummeting to the ground and she, her family, Will and thirty other people, including several staff, were all huddled under a canopy designed for six.

'Maybe we should make a run for it,' Lee suggested.

'Only if you fancy swimming without a swimming pool,' said Uncle Raymond, who was all for ordering drinks just to test if the waiters would fetch them in these conditions.

'He's right, you know,' Lee's dad said. 'We can't stand

here all day. If we go, the worst that can happen is that we'll get wet.'

'Very wet,' Lee's mum corrected. 'Wetter than a sponge immersed in water for twenty minutes. They'll still be squeezing us out when we get on the plane.'

So they waited another fifteen minutes … by which time the rain had been joined by lightning, which scorched the sky to the accompaniment of thunderous drum rolls.

'Well,' Lee's dad said. 'This just goes to show that it rains in Spain, too.' It was as if Lee's dad had been waiting for this moment – willing it, even – so that he could gain forgiveness for having taken them all on that wetter-than-wet camping holiday a year ago. 'It doesn't matter where you are, there's no guarantee you'll get decent weather.'

'We are *not* going camping again next year,' Lee's mum stated emphatically. 'At least we've had six days of good weather here and one – in fact, not even one, just a half – of rain. Last year it was the exact opposite.'

'But we saw a lot of nature last year.'

'Yes, that's right. Most of it was pouring into that stupid leaky tent you borrowed!'

Lee's dad gave up on this argument because there was no way he could win it; plus, he was outnumbered four to one by those who'd been there and experienced for themselves the misery of camping in a monsoon.

The rain continued to fall, bouncing off the ground around them and soaking their legs. The restaurant's roof was made of reeds and was completely useless. It would keep out bird droppings but that was about it. The rain seeped straight through.

'This rain isn't going to stop,' Uncle Raymond decided. 'We could be here all night. Which would be fine if they were serving up something tasty, like a big steak with lots of fries and veggies, but at this rate they won't be serving up anything at all.'

'Apart from water,' Lee's dad said. 'As much as you can drink.'

After another five minutes, everyone accepted that they were going to have to make a run for their hotels. Even Lee's mum was in agreement, because by then the canopy they were standing under was so wet that it was letting a good proportion of the rain soak straight through.

'Okay, okay,' she said. 'I don't suppose we have any choice unless we want to stand out here all night.'

They held their possessions close to them and Lee's dad began the countdown. 'Five, four …' Everyone joined in for the rest: 'Three, two, one, go!'

Five drowned rats arrived back at the hotel.

The men and boys had stripped off their tops, reckoning that if they were going to get wet anyway, they might as well not suffer having their soaked T-shirts clinging to their bodies. Even Lee's mum, who normally wouldn't go anywhere other than the beach or poolside with just her bikini on, saw the sense in wearing the minimum possible.

But being back in their hotel room didn't mean they were in the dry. Far from it. As they opened the door to their apartment, they were greeted by a lake that had formed in the hallway and had spread to the kitchen, bathroom, lounge and both bedrooms. On closer inspection (achieved by wading through the water) the inward-sloping balcony was revealed as the source of the problem. It was under several inches of water, which had made its way over the runners of the sliding doors and into the apartment proper. Everything that was touching the ground was saturated. If they'd had an inflatable dinghy they could have rowed it from room to room.

Lee's mum was distraught. 'This is a disaster! Look at all our stuff!' Predictably, the kids' room was, eh, let's just say not as tidy as it might have been. Clothes, bags, shoes, towels and everything else imaginable had been left lying around and it was all soaked through. Lee's mum and dad's room had, by comparison, been virtually spotless, but they'd still left their suitcases on the floor, so the contents were now wringing. Rummaging through their case, Lee's mum suddenly declared, 'I haven't got a single dry, clean pair of knickers!' Everyone fell silent. This was rather more than they needed to know.

'Eh, so, will you have to, you know, eh, stick a dirty pair back on tomorrow?' Uncle Raymond asked.

Lee's mum refused to answer.

They did their best to clean up, but what they really needed was a sponge the size of a swimming pool, and unfortunately the hotel didn't have any of those handy, so they had to make do with mops and buckets. The hotel staff did their best, but lots of other rooms were affected just as badly and they couldn't attend to everyone at the same time.

After a couple of hours of mopping up they decided to go and eat. Except that nearly all the outdoor restaurants were flooded out of use and all the indoor ones had been booked by holidaymakers with the foresight to realise what would happen as a result of the torrential rain. And so, for their last dinner, which was supposed to have been a slap-up eat-whatever-you-want meal, they ended up having bread and cheese, bought from a nearby shop and eaten in the hotel bar.

'Well at least all that water should have drowned a few of those ugly cockroaches,' Lee's mum said, looking on the bright side. 'Or can they swim …?' she added worriedly.

Whereas the adults were starting to concentrate on the practicalities of the journey home, Lee and Will still had important business to resolve.

They were the first to arrive at the Space Invaders machine, their designated meeting point. No one was playing it, so Will had a go while they were waiting. He was just about to achieve his highest score of the week when a girl said, 'Hi.' He looked up, saw Anna and, in doing so, missed a bomb falling from an alien space-ship, which proceeded to blow up his last remaining craft. 'Aghh!' he cried, causing Lee to jump in alarm.

'What is it?' he asked. 'Did you see them?'

'No, don't be so jumpy. I just lost my last guy.'

Lee breathed a sigh of relief. His nerves were on edge, but then no wonder, this could be a dangerous mission they were embarking on and the safety of all seven of them would rest on his shoulders. Maybe they were biting off more than they could chew?

No, he had to be confident. It was his job as a leader to look like he knew what he was doing, even if he had no plan whatsoever.

It wasn't long before Carmel, Padraig and Paula arrived together, followed by Ben, who had been told he needed to finish writing his postcards before he could wander off. He was a little out of breath as he rushed over to the others.

'I sorry,' he puffed. 'Are we go now, yes?'

'Well, there's no time like the present,' Lee told him.

Ben was baffled, but followed behind anyway, confident that all would become clear.

They arrived at the top of the stairs just in time to see a heavily built man thrusting a compact battering ram against a door. Peering around the corner, the gang of seven could see he was not alone. A woman and six other men were lined up ready to pile in to the room as soon as the door gave in, which wouldn't be long given the abuse it was getting.

'Isn't that the room Mr Shiny went into when we followed him?' Will asked Lee.

'It is,' Lee told him. 'And I reckon at least one of them must be in there.'

A crash announced that the door had just lost its fight. The man with the battering ram stood aside as the others charged into the room, shouting instructions as they did so. Only once they were all in did he follow on.

The moment the entire assault team was inside, the door to room 1066 swung open. Out strode a stranger, a man neither Lee nor Will recognised. He was moving with a sense of purpose.

'Who's that?' Anna whispered. Given all the noise from the room that was now without a door, only Lee heard her.

'I've no idea …'

But then suddenly he did. He knew exactly who it was. He wasn't wearing his flat cap, and gone were his expensive clothes, but it was very definitely …

Will was just as shocked. 'Perfect Father!' he realised.

'In disguise,' Padraig joined in. 'Like a spy.'

'Or a baddie,' Paula pointed out.

'Crikey,' Lee gasped. 'So he is. And he's trying to escape. We've got to stop him!'

By this time Perfect Father was almost at the top of the stairs from where the seven of them were watching what was going on.

'Block him,' Lee commanded and stood up right in front of Perfect Father as he was about to round the corner of the stairs.

'Out of the way!' Perfect Father yelled.

'Oh no you don't,' Will stated, with a slight quiver in his voice as he stood up next to Lee and blocked the way.

'Yeah,' Padraig cried. 'Stick 'em up. You'll need to get past us first before you can escape.'

'I've got a blue belt in Taekwando,' Lee warned Perfect Father as he started to move forward. 'And I'm licensed to use it.'

'Move. Quickly! Or you'll get seriously hurt. Can't you see there's a raid going on in there.' He pushed into the space between Lee and Will, but Ben and Anna immediately filled it. Paula grabbed one of Perfect Father's legs, then Padraig grabbed the other. 'Oh no you don't,' he cried.

'Get off. Get out of the way,' Perfect Father was shouting, but Carmel had joined the fray and jumped onto his back. It forced him to bend, allowing Lee and Will to grab an arm each, Lee trying to execute a Chinese burn at the same time as bending the man's arm.

They were all so engrossed in stopping Perfect Father that they didn't notice Perfect Mother until she too was at the top of the stairs. 'John!' she cried. 'What's …?'

Perfect Mother wasn't perfect any more. Her hair was tied in a bunch at the back of her head and was dark brown instead of fake blonde.

'Get them off me,' Perfect Father yelled back. 'Before those dealers get away.'

The door to Room 1066 opened again and out came Perfect Son and Perfect Daughter. Except that *they* weren't perfect any more either. Perfect Daughter no longer held her nose so high that passersby could see right up her nostrils, and her trendy jeans had … surely not … holes in them! Perfect Son had swapped his old-fashioned attire for a cool T-shirt, complete with skull and cross bones, and combat trousers, which looked to have at least five hundred pockets.

A surprisingly agile Perfect Mother grabbed Carmel around the waist and tried to pull her back to the ground. Meanwhile, Perfect Son and Perfect Daughter looked really annoyed that this group of youngsters was attacking their father.

This was going to be a tricky moment for Lee, Will and the others. Seven of them against two adults and two children. It would be close.

And then two things happened at exactly the same time. First, Uncle Raymond appeared around the corner of the staircase. He was leaping up the stairs, almost out of breath. Seeing that Lee and his friends were in trouble he bent over like a prop forward and readied himself for the scrum. 'Yaaaahhh,' he cried as he went to pile in.

However, the other thing that happened was someone shouted from along the corridor, 'It's okay! We've got them!'

Uncle Raymond pulled up short as the Perfects relaxed and Perfect Father stopped struggling so much.

'What's the story?' Uncle Raymond demanded in his gruffest voice.

'This lot,' Perfect Father muttered, 'almost ruined a crucial drugs bust.' He was able to stand straight again as Carmel relaxed her hold in the face of less resistance. 'That's the story. They could easily have escaped down the outside of the building and I needed to stop them. Only this lot decided that they knew better.'

'You mean …' Lee began.

But Paula was ahead of him. 'Are you really a goody then?'

'Spot on,' Perfect Mother told her firmly.

'And those guys …?' Will pointed up the corridor to the door.

'Those guys are big-time drug dealers who almost got away because of your interfering.'

'Hey, come on, no harm's been done,' Uncle Raymond said. 'You've got the guys you wanted and everyone's unhurt, that's the most important thing.'

'Yeah,' Lee said, thinking that it was always good to get your excuses in early and this seemed like the perfect moment. 'How were we supposed to know what you were up to? You've been sneaking around all week, not speaking to anyone …'

Will helped him out. '… Making Amador change the music down at the pool, nicking our sunloungers …'

Perfect Mother shook her head and jogged along to the smashed-down doorway. Her hair even moved freely and she no longer looked to have a pole stuck to her back keeping her head up and nose in the air.

'Anyway, what we're saying is …'

'… You could have told us,' Padraig finished for them. 'Wait until we tell our da we were in on a drugs bust!'

Carmel was less certain. 'He'll be worried that we could have got hurt.'

'And so he should be,' Perfect Father told her.

'You have got your children with you,' Anna pointed out, indicating Perfect Son and Perfect Daughter a few metres away in the corridor.

'That's different. They're …'

But he didn't finish his sentence because Perfect Mother called down from the flattened door, 'Coming out. Get the kids out of the way.'

'Right you lot, scarper,' Perfect Father instructed.

Uncle Raymond turned and led the way back down the stairs. 'Come on then. Sounds as if you've been involved in enough already.'

Lee insisted that they see the drug dealers being marched out of the hotel. It was too good a spectacle to miss. And Uncle Raymond relented, mainly because he was keen to see the whole thing for himself. 'To think all that was going on while we were here,' he mused.

Perfect Son and Perfect Daughter were first to appear in the lobby. A minute later the two men in shiny suits exited the lifts flanked by Perfect Father, Perfect Mother and the group that had stormed into the bedroom. The prisoners looked a good deal less full of themselves now. They hung their heads forward as if they thought that would hide their faces. Even their suits seemed duller than before, but then the prospect of a long spell in prison always takes the shine off a day.

Both were handcuffed and were distinctly unhappy about it. The calm Spaniard wasn't so calm any more. He ranted non stop. Lee thought it was probably just as well he was yelling in Spanish. He could imagine from the man's tone that the language being used was not the sort his mum and dad would want him to hear.

Perfect Father winked at Perfect Son and Perfect Daughter. Perfect Mother gestured that she would be back in a couple of minutes and that the Perfect Kids should remain where they were until then.

Will was intrigued by the transformation of Perfect Son and Perfect Daughter and shuffled over a few paces to where they were standing. 'Eh, how come you two haven't got posh accents any more?' he asked brashly.

'Oh that,' Perfect Son said, laughing ever so slightly. 'It was because of the drugs.'

'The drugs gave you a posh accent?' Lee queried. 'I know science has come on a long way, but ...'

'Because of the drugs *bust*,' Perfect Son told him.

'Aw.'

'A drugs bust that was almost a disaster. You guys very nearly blew our cover.'

'Yeah,' his sister said. 'You nearly messed things up big time.'

'Us?' Lee said, doing his best to look entirely innocent. 'How come?'

'Snooping around the place, coming up to our room with that stupid Christmas carol nonsense and everything.' Lee blushed as Perfect Daughter carried on. 'Dad did his nut. He even got you lot checked out in case you were somehow in on the whole thing.'

'Well how were we to know?' Will said. 'Those voices you put on, and the way you acted ...'

'We had to be convincing,' Perfect Daughter said. 'They wouldn't feel threatened if they thought that the people in the room next to them were just stupid, harmless toffs.'

'And then that time when we were down at the side of the pool and mum and dad were listening in on what was going on in the room ...'

'Using a bugging device?' Will asked.

'Yes. And then those Irish kids jumped in the pool and the spray they sent up stopped Dad's equipment working properly.'

'Was that the time when you insisted on taking our sunloungers?'

'We had to. We needed the metal in the legs to act as an aerial.'

'Aw,' Lee said, feeling more sheepish than a person with a very woolly jersey with *I Am A Sheep* written across the front in bold letters.

'And then on top of that there was the time down on the beach when we were using the poles of our windbreak as aerials and then suddenly and inexplicably the whole thing fell over, just when we were listening to a particularly important conversation ...'

Lee tried to move the conversation along. 'Eh, so who are those guys you were listening to?'

'Drug dealers,' Perfect Son told him. 'Big-time deal-ers who have helped ruin thousands of lives. They've been using that same hotel room for quite some time to negotiate deals, split the money and check drug samples.'

'The hotel manager is in on it too,' Will said. 'Although he doesn't want to be.'

'Why do you say that?'

'Lee overheard him talking with the other two.' Will looked at Lee. 'Didn't you.'

Lee nodded. 'He wanted them to stop using the hotel, but they just ignored him.'

'Hmm. I'll let Mum and Dad know about that.'

'So do you work for the police?' Will asked.

'No,' Perfect Son said.

'The government?'

'We don't work for anyone.'

'We just helped our parents this once,' Perfect Daugh-ter said. 'To make it look as if we were on a normal fam-ily summer holiday.'

'I wish our normal family summer holiday included being driven around in a Rolls Royce by a chauffeur,' Lee said.

'That was only so Mum and Dad would look the part when they turned up at a fancy party those guys were going to. They dropped us off with the other guy …'

'The guy in the Ferrari?' Will interrupted.

'Yes. Although it's a very old one.'

'Even so …'

'And it only has two seats, so we didn't actually get to go anywhere in it, we just got to sit in it and then went for dinner with the man who owns it. He's one of Dad's associates.'

'Who do your parents work for then?'

'They work for the government.'

'Secret Intelligence, more like, yeah?'

'Can't say.'

'Because it's secret,' Will pointed out.

'And I don't know anyway,' Perfect Son said. 'They're not allowed to tell us.'

'So your dad is like … James Bond.'

Perfect Son shrugged.

'How cool is that?!' Will was excited. 'Does he bring home loads of gadgets, like pens that fire torpedoes and umbrellas that turn into helicopters?'

'If he does, he doesn't leave them lying around the house,' Perfect Daughter said.

'Hadn't we better get back?' Will asked Lee. 'Your parents will be wondering where we've got to.'

Later, over their last dinner of the holiday, Lee was able to tell his dad some of what had gone on. Uncle Raymond had suggested to Lee that it would be better for his mum and dad's nerves if he and Will made out that they'd only seen the part of the whole episode in which the two drug dealers had been led out of the hotel, rather than saying that they'd made a point of trying to be where the real action was.

'The Perfects aren't snobs at all,' Lee told his dad. They've been having us all on.'

'If they're that good at acting they should be on stage.'

'Seemed to me as if they were relishing the role rather too much,' Lee's mum added.

Lee thought about this. Was his mum right? Had the Perfects taken advantage of their cover? What would he have done if told to play the part of a rich family on holiday?

And he decided that there was some truth in what his mum had said. Yes, it would have been fantastic to have been driven around in a Rolls Royce and to have had lots of expensive clothes to wear, but having a lot of money (or even pretending to have a lot of it) didn't mean you had to be rude or nasty or ignorant to other people. It was something Lee made a mental note of. If he ever became rich he would try to make sure that he was still nice to people. Being rich and being a snob were completely different things.

GOING HOME

When the bus arrived and ferried them out to the airport the sky was still grey. That made it less of a wrench to leave the resort behind because being in a sunshine resort wasn't much fun when there wasn't any sunshine.

From the moment they took off, everything went surprisingly smoothly: a tailwind meant the plane was able to make up some of the lost time; the lunch they were served was actually edible; and Lee didn't need the toilet the whole way back. Better still, their seats were just one row behind those of the Perfect Family, which was brilliant because Lee and Will were able to ping pieces of paper at them and then feign innocence by staring intently at their books. Their deviousness was never discovered.

They were surprised to find Uncle Raymond's partner, Liz, waiting for them outside Lee's family's house. She was dressed in jeans and a green wax jacket, but at least this time when rejoining civilisation she'd left her wellies at home.

'What are *you* doing here?' Lee's mum asked, giving her a hug.

'I just thought I'd come and welcome you back home,' Liz said, all smiles. Uncle Raymond gave her a big sloppy kiss as well as a hug, while Lee and Will looked away at a brick wall that was suddenly very interesting.

Lee's dad opened the door and they all piled into the house, Liz forging ahead. 'So, how was your holiday?' she asked, walking straight down the hall and into the kitchen.

Lee knew it was a good thing that Liz felt at home in their house, but on this occasion she seemed *too* at home.

Then he saw why.

So did the others. Because through the patio doors they could all see that the garden had disappeared! Gone was the not-very-good grass that was more moss than grass, and gone were the weed-filled beds that possibly had flowers hidden somewhere in them; gone also (thankfully) was the smashed-up greenhouse in the corner beside the tree; in fact, gone was the tree!

'Someone's stolen our garden!' Rebecca cried.

Liz flung open the patio doors, which she had obviously left unlocked. Lee stepped out first, with his mum and dad and Rebecca right behind him. 'Oh my goodness!' Lee's mum gasped, while his dad was speechless. So was Lee until he walked forward to the edge of the extension. Suddenly, out of the corner of his eye, he detected movement. A body! A man hiding under the kitchen window!

He did what any fit kid with an above-average reaction time and a blue belt in Taekwando would do – he lashed out with both fists whilst executing a near-perfect flying sidekick and shouting 'Asha!'. Lee's instructor would have been proud of him.

It wasn't, however, what the man had been expecting as he'd stepped forward, closely followed by a cameraman. It hurt the man when Lee caught him slap-bang (and thwack-thud) in the stomach with the hard, bony part of his foot, closely followed by the equally hard, bony part of his right fist. The man staggered back, tripped over the cameraman and landed in a very artistic water feature.

'Lee!' Liz screamed.

'Don't worry,' Lee called. 'I'll protect you!' And he

stepped forward to finish the man off.

'No!' Liz yelled.

'No!' Lee's mum yelled, too, having worked out what was going on.

'No!' the man yelled, backing off as fast as he could.

A very short, glamorous young woman suddenly appeared. Her hands were clean and smooth, a clear indication that she spent all her time bossing people about rather than actually doing any real work. 'Hello!' she greeted them all as warmly as possible.

'Who are you?' Lee demanded to know. 'Put your hands on your head and don't make a move! And you,' he commanded the cameraman, 'put that gun down.'

'It's a camera, Lee!' Liz said stepping forward just as Lee was preparing to execute an axe kick. 'These people have done up your garden while you've all been on holiday. I asked them to – as a special surprise!'

Now that he was certain his family would be safe and he no longer needed to protect them, Lee was beginning to recognise the faces before him. 'Aw,' he said. 'Sorry, I thought you were burglars.'

The woman bounced over to Lee's mum and dad. 'Hi, I'm Titchy Almarsh, from Garden Doer-Uppers. So what do you think of your new back garden?' she asked.

'I can't believe it,' Lee's mum said. 'It's lovely!'

'It's amazing,' Lee's dad agreed. 'We always meant to do it up but never got round to it.'

Liz grinned so broadly at their delight that it looked for a moment as if she might swallow her own head. There were tears of happiness in her eyes.

Rebecca also had tears in her eyes. 'Bring us our old garden back,' she cried. 'I want our scruffy old garden.'

The male presenter squelched over, clearly believing that the show must go on, even if you've just fallen into a water feature and your jeans are sticking to your legs so tightly that you can hardly move. 'Hi, I'm Wally Talsh.' Wally held out his hand. Lee's mum and dad shook it, then wiped their hands dry on their trousers.

'Dad usually watches that other programme,' Rebecca told Wally.

Wally tried to laugh this off. 'I can't imagine which one that could be!'

So Rebecca explained. 'It's the one where every time the woman comes on Dad stops what he's doing.'

'Ha ha,' Wally said. 'Well hopefully he'll change channels from now on.'

Rebecca wasn't convinced. 'I doubt it,' she said.

'Anyway,' Wally carried on, turning to the camera. 'There we have it. Three days hard graft clearly very much appreciated by the Waters family. What was once a scruffy old back yard, all overgrown and badly looked after …'

'Hoy, it wasn't that bad!' Lee called over.

'… is now a beautiful, easy-to-maintain delight of a garden that the whole family can appreciate.'

Rebecca sidled up to him as he tried to continue talking. 'Hey Wally, where's my swing? I know it was old and rusty, but I loved my swing. I played on it every day and now it's gone.'

'We threw that old junk in a skip,' Wally told her out of the side of his mouth, hoping the microphone attached to the camera wouldn't pick up his words. 'With any luck it's in a landfill site by now.' He turned back to the camera and smiled. 'That's one of the things I love about this job: the gratitude we're shown when we've just done up someone's garden.' He reached over to the side of the house and produced a large bottle of champagne. 'Anyway, from all of us here with the ecstatic Waters family, until next time, goodbye.'

THE END

.

YOUR THOUGHTS

If you have any thoughts about this book, or if you simply want to complain about the jokes in it, please contact Keith via his website:

www.keithacharters.co.uk

where you can also get details on more books in the Lee series.

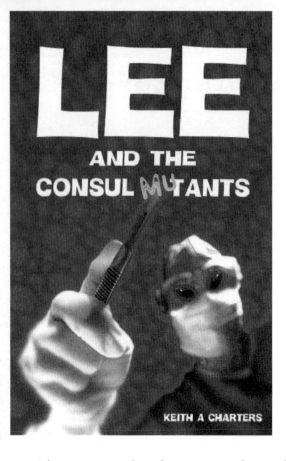

It's not every day that a part of your body explodes, but Lee's appendix does exactly that, landing him in hospital.

Soon after his operation, Lee is shocked to discover that evil Consul Mutants are trying to take over the world. Worse still, the hospital he is stuck in contains the portal they are using to invade Earth.

Other kids might quake in their boots at this news, but not Lee. He's determined to save the planet and comes up with a cunning plan to stop the aliens.

This is the story of a fearless boy battling against intergalactic odds for the sake of mankind. Lee's only weapon is his intelligence … which is a pity.

ISBN 1-903238-82-X

Meeting his dad's multizillionaire boss inspires Lee to come up with a get-rich-quick scheme of his own.

But not everyone is keen for Lee to succeed. Local shopkeeper Panface isn't, and it seems that he has sneaky spies out there, trying to ruin Lee's plans.

Will Lee get the better of his rivals? Or will he spend the whole time daydreaming about how many houses he'll own and how many butlers he'll have?

Lee will need to rely on his common sense and financial genius if he's to succeed in business … so it could be a struggle.

ISBN 1-905537-00-X